NIGHTMARE
AT THE MUSEUM

by
N.J. HUMPHREYS

Marshall Cavendish
Editions

Published by Marshall Cavendish Editions
An imprint of Marshall Cavendish International

A member of the
Times Publishing Group

Other Marshall Cavendish Offices:
Marshall Cavendish Corporation, 99 white Plains Road, Tarrytown NY 10591-9001, USA · Marshall Cavendish International (Thailand) Co Ltd, 253 Asoke, 12th Flr, Sukhumvit 21 Road, Klongtoey Nua, wattana, Bangkok 10110, Thailand · Marshall Cavendish (Malaysia) Sdn Bhd, Times Subang, Lot 46, Subang Hi-Tech Industrial Park, Batu Tiga, 40000 Shah Alam, Selangor Darul Ehsan, Malaysia.

Marshall Cavendish is a registered trademark of Times Publishing Limited

National Library Board, Singapore Cataloguing-in-Publication Data

Name(s): Humphreys, Neil.
Title: Nightmare at the museum / by N.J. Humphreys.
Other titles(s): Princess incognito.
Description: Singapore : Marshall Cavendish Editions, [2019]
Identifier(s): OCN 1129136756 | ISBN 978-981-48-6876-1 (paperback)
Subject(s): LCSH: Princesses--Juvenile fiction. | Family secrets--Juvenile fiction.
Classification: DDC 823.92--dc23

Printed in Singapore

Cover art and all illustrations by Cheng Puay Koon

For our favourite bus driver ... thanks mate.

INTRODUCTION TO ME AND MY BIG FAT LIE

My name is Sabrina Valence and I live a big fat lie. I'm 11 years old and I'm a princess. I'm serious. I'm not making this up. I'm not one of those soppy girls who fantasise about being a princess. I AM a princess. The trouble is, I'm a secret princess, which is a real pain in the backside.

My Uncle Ernie calls me "Princess Incognito", which sounds really daft. But then, Uncle Ernie is a bit daft. He's not even my real uncle. He's just mad. His real name is the Earl of Parslowe and he calls himself a "handyman". But I know what he really is.

He looks after me because I have no parents. All right, I do have parents but I never see them. I have to be careful what I write here because my eyes get all wet and sting-y when I think about my parents. I know I'm too old for all that weepy stuff, but even grown-ups cry when they lose their parents and I've lost mine.

And it's not even my fault.

It's the fault of dozy politicians who keep making the wrong decisions.

My official name is Princess Sabrina of Mulakating. I am the daughter of King Halbutt Valence and Queen Beverly Sisley. We are called the Royal House of Valence, which I was really proud of until my cousins starting calling us the Royal House of Flatulence.

Flatulence is a posh way of saying too much farting!

But I'd rather have a smelly surname than the life I live now. It really stinks. My mum and dad sent me away because Mulakating is having something called a "civil war", which is violent and dumb. Half of Mulakating wants to keep the royal family and the other half wants to get rid of us. They say we cost too much money and never do anything, which is crazy.

My mum and dad cut ribbons, shake hands and wave at people all day long!

But I was still kicked out of my own country. Daddy said he was saving my life. I think he was ruining my life.

I left my home, my friends and even Miss Quick-Pants. She was my teacher at the Palace. Her real name was Miss Cruickshanks, but the young royals all called her Miss Quick-Pants. But most of all, I had to leave my parents.

That was the worst moment of my life.

But at least I've got Uncle Ernie. He took me to a housing estate in a rough neighbourhood in the middle of nowhere and sent me to one of the worst schools in the world. We wear green blazers that look like vomit. We have a principal called the Cannibal. She doesn't eat people. Her real name is Miss Cannington, and the Cannibal is her nickname.

My teacher is called Miss Shufflebottom and that's not even her nickname.

Her actual name is Miss Shufflebottom!

Even a nickname couldn't be as funny as Miss Shufflebottom. I've told Uncle Ernie that he's not allowed to talk to her anymore because whenever he meets her, he says, "Hello, Miss Shufflebottom" and bursts out laughing!

Uncle Ernie has given me what he calls a "cover story". It's a made-up story about my fake life. I'm supposed to be this really boring, quiet girl from a really boring, quiet town and I live in a tiny house because my parents are working overseas. My previous life, my real life, no longer exists.

I spend all day telling lies, not little white lies, but ridiculous whoppers. I am the only 11-year-old in the world who gets told to tell lies and gets told off for telling the truth!

It's so confusing.

I can't tell anyone that I'm an expert in horse riding,

taekwondo and fencing and almost an expert in aikido. I can't say that I speak English, French, Spanish and some Mandarin. I can't say that I'm a princess in hiding, thousands of miles away from my parents and that sometimes, when I'm alone in my bedroom, my eyes start stinging and there's absolutely nothing I can do about it.

It's getting harder and harder to remember what is true and what is false.

At school, I have one friend, a tiny boy called Charlie. He knows I have secrets on the Internet so he thinks I'm a YouTube star!

And then there is Awful Agatha.

She's not as awful as she used to be, but she's still the school bully and most days can't remember if she likes me or not. She changes like the weather. She even likes being called Awful Agatha. I think she's getting suspicious about me though. She thinks I'm weird. And she's right. My life is weird.

That's why I keep this journal, just for me. This is the true story of a princess who cannot tell the truth, a princess with a terrible secret.

But today should be a good day.

Today, our class is going on a school field trip. We are off to the museum, which should be fun. I mean, it's a museum, right? What could possibly go wrong?

CHAPTER ONE

A funny little man stood up at the front of the school bus.

"My name is Alan," he said.

"Good morning, Mr Alan," everyone on the bus replied.

We were getting impatient. The bus hadn't even left the school yet because Liam wouldn't stop doing kick-ups with his new football. He was totally showing off in front of the girls, who kept giggling. I'm sure one of them had blown him a kiss.

Awful Agatha had blown him a raspberry.

By the time Miss Shufflebottom had shuffled everyone's bottoms onto the bus and confiscated Liam's football, we were already five minutes late.

And that's when the funny little man behind the steering wheel decided to stand up and give us a little speech.

"I am your bus driver today," said Alan.

"Good morning, Mr Alan the Bus Driver," we all shouted back, giggling.

"There's no need to call me Alan the Bus Driver. Just Alan will do."

"Good morning, Mr Just Alan Will Do," Awful Agatha said.

Miss Shufflebottom gave Awful Agatha one of her meanest stares. At least, Miss Shufflebottom thought she looked mean. No one else did.

Naturally, Awful Agatha didn't care. She never does. She was the meanest bully in the school and has already dragged me into two fights. But I wasn't scared. Uncle Ernie started teaching me taekwondo when I was four, back at the Palace.

Awful Agatha wasn't scared of anything either, except suspension. She never wanted to be sent home from school. She was strange. Every day, I think of ways to get back to my parents. Every day, Awful Agatha tries to think of ways to stay away from her parents.

So I knew she would be a million miles from caring when she made fun of Alan the Bus Driver. Even when Miss Shufflebottom and Miss Cannington stood behind him and pointed at Awful Agatha, she just slouched in her seat and chewed her gum.

In fact, Miss Shufflebottom and the old Cannibal made it even worse for poor Alan the Bus Driver. They were much taller than him, which made him look even funnier. It's really hard to concentrate when a big speech is coming from such a small man.

"Ok, boys and girls, now that I've got your attention, listen carefully," said Alan the Bus Driver. "Today, I'd really like to be something. What would I like to be?"

"Taller," shouted Awful Agatha.

Our giggling spread through the school bus. Even Miss Shufflebottom turned away.

Charlie was chuckling in the seat beside me and he didn't really like Awful Agatha, for two obvious reasons. First, he was much smaller and smarter than her, which are the two things that school bullies always seem to attack. And second, as my closest friend, he couldn't understand why I would be friendly with a girl like her.

But I had my reasons. Awful Agatha and I both had family secrets. That's why I was the only person on the school bus brave enough to do what I did next.

"All right, Agatha," I whispered.

We gazed at each other across the aisle of the school bus. She had dark rings under her eyes and those horrible yellow clumps of sleep in the corners of her eyes. Her long, black hair was shiny, but not in an attractive way. It was greasy and knotty. She hadn't been sleeping or washing properly, again.

"Are you telling me to shut up?" Agatha hissed at me.

"No, I just want him to start driving so we can eat our sandwiches. I'm starving already. Are you?"

Awful Agatha didn't say anything. But she pulled that unusual face, the one that only I saw, the one that made her look soft.

"Yeah, a little bit," she whispered.

"Me too," I said and then I waved at Alan the Bus Driver.

"Sorry about that, Mr Alan. Can we go now?"

"In a minute," the little man said.

And then he stared at me, for ages. It was really awkward.

"Have I seen you before?"

My cheeks were on fire. Most people, most normal people anyway, hear this question all the time. They're always bumping into people. They bump into each other at school, in the supermarket, on a train, on a bus, in the street, in the park, everywhere. But I don't bump into people. Ever. At the Palace, I was never allowed to bump into normal people because a princess was never allowed to go to normal places. Now, I don't bump into normal people outside of school because Uncle Ernie never allows his hidden princess to go to normal places. So when I'm recognised, I panic.

Being recognised by strangers can only mean one thing.

They know who I really am. They know I am Princess Sabrina Valence of Mulakating. And then my secret is out.

And then my life is in danger.

And Alan the Bus Driver had recognised me. It was *so* obvious.

Uncle Ernie wasn't sitting beside me with all his hidden gadgets to save me. Charlie was sitting beside me with all his detective maths puzzles. They wouldn't save me.

Liam was sitting behind me, burping. His burps wouldn't save me.

On the other side, Awful Agatha was clenching her fists, probably deciding which student she was going to punch later at the museum. Her fighting wouldn't save me.

I was on my own.

"No, I don't think so," I said.

Alan the Bus Driver wasn't convinced. He wandered down the aisle of the bus.

"Have you been on my bus before? I take students to the museum every day. Have you been on one of my school trips?"

"Er, yeah, maybe."

I thought my brain was going to explode and splatter against the bus window like cold porridge.

"You told me you've never been to this museum before," Charlie said.

"Shut up, Charlie."

Charlie was sweet and kind and almost cute with his short hair and glasses. But his mouth was always five seconds faster than his brain.

"Maybe I visited with my Uncle Ernie," I said. "I can't really remember."

"Yeah, nor can I," said Alan the Bus Driver.

I had done a brilliant job of confusing him. Another little white lie had saved me. I was turning into a fantastic liar.

Alan the Bus Driver returned to the front of the bus. It was hard to see him. His head only just poked out above our seats.

"Ok, I think we're ready to leave now," he said.

We all cheered.

"I just have one more thing to say."

We all booed.

"There is only one rule," said Alan the Bus Driver. "You must follow all my rules. That means no eating, no drinking, no shouting, no singing, no spitting, no swearing, no fighting, no wrestling, no nose-picking, finger-flicking, hair-pulling or clothes-ripping, no peeing, no pooing, no kissing, no wooing, no farting, no burping, no vomiting, no slurping and no talking, especially no talking, unless it's an emergency, like one of you is on fire or something. Apart from that, you can do whatever you want. So sit back, relax and enjoy your trip to the museum."

Charlie took a deep breath and raised his hand.

"Er, excuse me. Are we allowed to sleep?"

"Only if you don't snore."

Alan the Bus Driver sat behind his huge steering wheel. The old guy looked liked a baby in a toy car. He turned a key. Suddenly, the school bus was full of spitting, farting, burping and vomiting noises.

It was the engine!

The bus bounced away from the school like a dizzy kangaroo.

"Come on, you silly old girl, get us to the museum in one piece."

Alan the Bus Driver talked to his bus, as if the bus was a real person.

He made me laugh.

He saw me watching him, through that large mirror stuck to his windscreen.

"I've definitely seen you before," he said, peering over the top of his glasses. "By the end of today, I will remember who you are."

He made me stop laughing.

CHAPTER 2

There was no toilet! What kind of school bus doesn't have a toilet? My school bus, obviously. Back at the Palace, every room had its own toilet. Even Miss Quick-Pants had her own toilet, which no one else was allowed to use and no one else really wanted to use. She was old and smelly.

But we were young and smelly. Or at least, Liam and his childish friends were. Liam sat behind me on the bus, making all sorts of disgusting noises from different parts of his body. I knew what he was doing. The dukes and earls at the Palace used to do exactly the same thing.

Boys are *so* predictable.

He was trying to get my attention because he had a crush on me. At the Palace, the dukes and earls would get on their horses and leap the highest fences on our equestrian course. Or they would have a fencing fight in the main hall to impress me. Or they would score a great goal in polo.

On the school bus, Liam farted like a trumpet.

He tried to perform the school song just by making foul noises, which I thought was really disrespectful, not of the school song, but of everyone on the bus.

Liam stank.

And we had no toilet to escape to. Actually, we did. But Alan the Bus Driver had stuck an 'Out of Order' sign across the door and locked it, which was obviously a total lie. I'm an expert in lying. And Alan the Bus Driver was telling a huge one.

What's worse, Awful Agatha really needed to use the toilet, which was her own silly fault. She had stuffed her hungry face with too many of my sandwiches.

But that's all right. She didn't steal them.

We have a secret agreement. Uncle Ernie makes loads of extra cheese sandwiches for me to give to Awful Agatha because her parents don't seem to care about her that much and this makes her sad and angry and a bit of a bully. And she accepts my extra cheese sandwiches because my parents are not around and that makes me sad and angry and a bit lonely.

I'm still not sure how our secret agreement helps me, but I like making people happy in this miserable place.

It stops me thinking about all the family I left behind.

"Oi, Sabzy," Awful Agatha whispered, leaning over the aisle and into my seat.

She keeps trying to come up with cool nicknames for me because she thinks every kid should have a cool nickname and she keeps telling me that "Sabrina" sounds too posh and rich and not very "street".

I don't understand why my name should sound like a street, but I don't mind having a nickname. The problem is, well, Awful Agatha gets easily distracted. That's what Miss Shufflebottom wrote on her last school report. She was "easily distracted". Uncle Ernie said she was as thick as two short planks.

That's a bit unfair. But Awful Agatha can be forgetful. She forgets the nicknames she gives me.

"Sabs, Sabs, don't ignore me, Sabs," she said.

But Charlie was already ignoring her. Like I said, he can't understand why I'm friendly with the worst bully in the worst school. So he stared out of the window, which seemed pointless. Every council house looks the same in our town. People are weirdos here. They like to leave their indoor furniture outdoors. There are always old sofas and washing machines outside the houses.

"Sabs, don't turn your back on me, Sabs."

Awful Agatha wouldn't leave me alone.

"What do you want?"

"I need to go to the toilet."

I looked over at Awful Agatha. She was gripping the sides of the seat and gritting her teeth, as if she was getting ready for another fight in the playground.

"We haven't got a toilet. You'll have to hold it until we get to the museum."

"I can't."

"Then pee in your water bottle."

"It's not that kind of toilet."

I felt Charlie shaking beside me. He was grinning. Big mistake.

"Is he laughing at me? Oi, midget, are you laughing at me?"

Charlie bit his bottom lip and turned around. His face was redder than a traffic light. He had been totally laughing. And he couldn't quite stop. He had the giggles.

"No, no, I'm not laughing."

"Sabzy, tell Charlie to stop laughing."

"Charlie, stop laughing."

But Charlie couldn't help himself. His face was turning from red to purple, like our painting palettes in our art classes, where we add darker colours to make different shades. Charlie was now a darker shade of purple and his cheeks were ready to pop.

"I'm sorry, but you need to do a poo poo!"

Charlie exploded this time. Some of his saliva landed on my ugly green blazer. Charlie is my kindest friend, but he can be so childish sometimes.

"You're being an idiot," I said. "Stop laughing or I won't talk to you."

But Charlie didn't listen. He was out of control.

Awful Agatha stood up and leaned right across my seat and into Charlie's face.

"Stop laughing or I'll punch you in the face."

Charlie controlled himself.

He went back to staring at the council houses through the window and I returned to Awful Agatha's bulging stomach.

"Why did you eat the sandwiches so quick, Agatha?"

"I always have an early lunch."

"It's nine-thirty in the morning."

"All right, Mrs Stopwatch! I eat early and then I'm full for the rest of the day."

"So you are full now?"

"Not really. Can I have another sandwich?"

"Agatha!"

Suddenly, we all fell forward. Alan the Bus Driver slammed

on the brakes. Awful Agatha tapped her forehead on the back of the seat in front of her.

"Ow! What's he doing? Does he want me to go to the toilet in one of his seats, because I will, you know, I will! I don't care."

"I think the coach is smelly enough," I said, before raising my voice until it was really loud, "thanks to Liam!"

"I heard that," he shouted over my chair.

And then he burped. He's such a fool. Some of the girls really like him. They think he's handsome and funny and good at football and say he looks a bit like that young actor who plays Spiderman. They both have black hair, although Liam's hair is floppy because he keeps a long fringe. And they are both short. But that's it. Spiderman doesn't make rude noises to impress the girls, does he?

I wasn't interested in Liam's rubbish, even if he was handsome and funny and rather good at football. That's according to the other girls, by the way, not me, or Awful Agatha. I haven't got time for boys at the moment and Awful Agatha dislikes anyone who doesn't give her cheese sandwiches.

But apart from Liam's flirting and Awful Agatha's toilet talk, I was really looking forward to visiting the museum. I like history and wars—apart from history and wars that involve my family—and this was my first school trip with Charlie.

I was going to try really hard not to think about my family and enjoy the day.

Alan the Bus Driver stood up. He was carrying a pile of leaflets.

"Sorry about the jerking," he said. "The old girl has had it. Needs new brakes. Filter. Oil change. The lot. The guts have gone."

We had absolutely no idea what he was going on about.

"Anyway, welcome to the Mayesbrook Museum of Modern and Ancient Wonders," said Alan the Bus Driver, handing out leaflets down the aisle.

"This is a map of all the attractions. The tour guide will give you all the details, but my favourites are the Planetarium, where you'll learn about the solar system and the Chamber of Nightmares, which is always scary fun."

"I'll have a nightmare on this bus if you don't let me off to use the toilet," said Awful Agatha, snatching a map.

"Yes, you can get off when you've got a leaflet," said Alan the Bus Driver, handing maps to Charlie and me. "And they've also got a new exhibition on royal families, showing powerful, young princesses from all over the world."

And I knew, straightaway, that today was going to be one of the worst days of my life.

CHAPTER THREE

Miss Cannington made us wait outside the museum with the pigeons. The museum was a huge, grey building with towering pillars. There was a long, stone staircase that ran all the way from the street—which seemed miles away—to the museum entrance. I wanted to sit down, but the concrete steps were freezing and there was pigeon poop everywhere.

We had to stand together so Miss Shufflebottom could count all the students. Apparently, regular teachers always count their students when they go on school trips, just in case they lose any.

"It's true," Charlie whispered, as he tucked his detective maths puzzle book under his arm.

"What's true?"

"What Miss Shufflebottom just said about losing students. Last year, before you came to our school, we went to a city farm and lost Awful Agatha."

"Wow, really? How?"

"Sausages."

"What?"

"Sausages. When we saw the pigs behind the fence, the farmer told us that pigs came from sausages. So she jumped over the fence."

"Why?"

"She said she wanted a sausage for her sandwich."

"But that's crazy."

"Not really. She only had bread and butter."

"Was it dangerous?" I asked.

"Only for the pigs."

"She was ok with the pigs?"

"Yeah, she was fine. We found her two hours later. She was lying on some straw, between two pigs."

"Was she upset?"

"Nah. She said it was her best school day ever."

Miss Shufflebottom tapped our heads as she counted, just to make sure she didn't miscount.

"That's 18, 19, 20, 21 and ... there's no 22. Where is number 22? Who is number 22? Who's missing?"

She spun around so many times, I thought her head was going to come off.

"Who's missing? I can't see ... wait ... where's Agatha? It's not Agatha, not again, where's Agatha? Where's Agatha?"

Miss Shufflebottom hopped up and down the stone steps like one of the pigeons.

"It's ok, Miss Shufflebottom," I said. "Agatha went to the toilet with Miss Cannington."

"Oh, thank heavens for that," she muttered. "I hope this museum doesn't have a pig farm."

"No, no, it doesn't have a pig farm, I can assure you."

We all looked up to see where the posh, slightly whiny voice was coming from. At the top of the stairs, a tall, skinny man pointed a long, bony finger in our direction. He stood beside a shorter, much younger man, maybe even a teenager. They both wore the same light green museum uniforms, even lighter than our vomit-coloured school blazers. Our blazers looked like sick. Their bright green uniforms made me feel sick.

We moved up to the stair below the two strange men, which meant I could see right up the taller man's long nose. It was very thin and straight and pointy, like a snowy ski slope. When he breathed, his nostrils vibrated and his nose hairs danced from side to side.

I was a bit worried about Charlie. He was so small and the man's nose was so big that if he took a really deep breath, he might suck poor Charlie into a jungle of snot.

"Good morning, boys and girls," he said. "I will be your museum guide today."

"Yeah, hur hur, he's your museum guide today," said the shorter one beside him.

"My name is Mr Cumberlatch," the taller man continued. "It's quite a hard name to pronounce, so let's say it together, shall we? Repeat after me … Cumber."

"Cumber," we all shouted on the museum steps.

"Latch," he said.

"Latch," we all repeated.

"Excellent, put them together and it's Cumberlatch," he said.

"Cumberlatch," we all replied.

"Cabbage patch," said Awful Agatha.

She was back and already causing mischief. She stood beside me and grinned.

"Good one, right? Do you get it?"

"That's enough Agatha," Miss Cannington said, already red-faced, already embarrassed, already annoyed with Awful Agatha.

Here's the thing about the old Cannibal.

She's quite a kind woman, really, for a headmistress anyway. But she panics too much. Being a royal, I'm trained not to panic. Uncle Ernie teaches me loads of cool things to think and do in a crisis. But our headmistress has never had crisis training before. And she sometimes makes a crisis out of nothing. Or sometimes, she tries to fix a problem and ends up making it worse.

"I'm so sorry about Agatha," she said to the museum guide. "She can occasionally say the wrong thing or pronounce a word incorrectly, Mr Cumbersnatch."

Mr Cumberlatch squeezed his face.

"It's Mr Cumberlatch, actually."

"Of course it is, I'm so sorry. I feel terrible, Mr Lumbercatch. Latch! I mean, latch, like the latch of a door, ha ha! Not catch like a ball, no, not a ball, you're not a ball, you're a latch, which goes with the, er, cumber, as in cucumber, not that you're a cucumber. I'm not saying that you are a cucumber, even though your uniform is green and you are very long. But you're not a cucumber, no, not at all. Just cumber and latch, put together, almost like Cumberland, like Cumberland sausage. Do you like Cumberland sausages? Yes, we all do, don't we? I know Agatha does because last year, she went looking for sandwiches in the ... the ... sorry, where was I?

Sausages! That's it. Cumberland, no, not Cumberland, Cumberlatch, that's right, Cumberlatch, so, that's it. Yes. I'm glad we got that all sorted out. Good. I'll let you carry on, Mr Crumblebatch."

"IT'S MR CUMBERLATCH," we all shouted.

"Ah, listen to my lovely students, they're an enthusiastic bunch, aren't they?"

The old Cannibal's face was now the colour of a strawberry sundae.

"Yes, I can see where they get it from," Mr Cumberlatch said, blowing his nose with a hankie that looked bigger than a bed sheet.

"Now, as I was saying, I am your tour guide. And this is Bonzo."

"Yeah, I'm Bonzo, hur hur," said the younger, fidgety guide in a really deep voice.

He started waving at us.

"I'm Bonzo, hur hur. Can you all see me?"

He was still waving at us.

"Yes, thank you, Bonzo. Bonzo is my assistant tour guide."

"Yeah, I'm his assistant, hur hur. Can you all see me?"

He was still waving at us!

Mr Cumberlatch shook his head.

"Yes, put your hand down, Bonzo, they can see who you are. Ok, if you'd like to follow me into one of the best museums in the country."

"Yeah, one of the best museums in the country," Bonzo said.

Everyone pushed and shoved each other to get into the museum. The stone pillars towered over our heads as we headed inside.

Some students screamed as they ran into a hairy elephant.

"Ah, this is our mascot," said Mr Cumberlatch.

"No, it's an elephant. *Duh*," Awful Agatha said.

Mr Cumberlatch laughed, but it was obviously one of those fake laughs that I do with Uncle Ernie when he tells his lame knock-knock jokes.

"Ha ha, that's very funny," said Mr Cumberlatch.

"Yeah, ha ha, very funny," said Bonzo.

"Thank you, Bonzo. No, a mascot is like a lucky charm. And this woolly mammoth has stood at the entrance of our museum ever since we opened. It lived during the last ice age."

Charlie raised his hand. "Has your museum been open since the last ice age?"

I gave Charlie a gentle nudge in the ribs, not enough to hurt him, just enough to stop him asking silly questions.

"No, it's not been around that long. Ok, open up your maps."

Awful Agatha shared my map. She had used hers as a paper aeroplane and thrown it at Liam's head.

"Stop shaking the map," she hissed. "I can't read as well as you."

But it wasn't my fault. My hands were shaking. My eyes were stinging. I was seconds away from seriously panicking. I watched Awful Agatha's finger follow the different exhibitions as Mr Cumberlatch spoke.

It was getting really hard to see the words on the map, or even hear the words coming out of Mr Cumberlatch's mouth.

The museum exhibitions are shaped like a spider's web and blah, blah, blah.

There is the Planetarium with stars and blah, blah, blah.

There is the Chamber of Nightmares with scary stuff and Tombs of Ancient Egypt with dead stuff and blah, blah, blah.

And in the middle of the spider's web is the Royalty Exhibition, which focuses on princesses, because of equality and because of women being as important as men and all that other empowering stuff.

Princess Power is in the middle of the Royalty Exhibition, which is in the middle of the daft spider's web, which is in the middle of everything.

Princess Power.

I mean, really, *Princess Power.*

That's what the Royalty Exhibition was called.

Stupid name. Stupid idea.

I couldn't think. I couldn't breathe.

And then the Cabbage Patch said something that made the woolly mammoth spin around the grand entrance of the museum.

"Don't worry, we are just like modern superhero movies. We don't just focus on powerful men," he said. "We also focus on young, independent women. We've got lots of cool stuff on princesses from big countries like England and Japan and smaller places like Monaco and Mulakating."

And that's when I fainted.

CHAPTER FOUR

When I woke up, I saw stars. Real stars. There were actual stars above my head. There were also eyes, so many scary-looking eyes, staring right into my face.

At first, I thought I was dreaming. In my dreams, I always saw Mummy and Daddy. But these eyes didn't belong to my parents.

Plus, I recognised that ski-slope nose.

"Oh, thank heavens, she's awake. I can't have any more disasters on school trips."

That was Miss Cannington's voice.

"Tell me about it. I still have nightmares about pig farms."

That was Miss Shufflebottom's voice.

"I have never had a student faint in my museum before."

That was Mr Cumberlatch's voice.

"I can see a big bogey up her nose."

That was Awful Agatha's voice.

This was definitely not a dream. I was back in my museum nightmare.

In the sky above, the stars twinkled. The sky was black. How long had I been asleep for? I was going nuts.

I pointed up at the sky. My arm was shaking.

"Is it night time?"

I heard the teachers laugh, but it wasn't a real laugh. It

was one of those nervous laughs that grown-ups do when they're embarrassed.

"No, it's still the morning," Miss Cannington said. "You only fainted for a moment or two. So we brought you into the Planetarium."

"One of the best planetariums in the world," said Mr Cumberlatch.

"Yeah, one of the best planetariums in the world."

"Shut up, Bonzo," said Mr Cumberlatch. "Now, young lady, the next Planetarium show is about to start in ten minutes. Would you like to see our nurse, have a glass of water and stay, or would you like to go home?"

Suddenly, I remembered everything. I remembered the Cabbage Patch going on and on about his fancy royal exhibition and his silly Princess Power display. And then I heard him mention Mulakating, my home, my Mummy and Daddy's home, where the people love me, or used to love me, or some of them love me and some of them hate me, or hate the royal family, or something. I didn't know anything anymore, except for one thing. I couldn't be recognised, not here.

If I was spotted next to the rotten exhibition about my own family, I'd be dead.

Even Uncle Ernie wouldn't be able to rescue me.

"Go home," I said, so loudly that I made Miss Shufflebottom jump. I sat up and saw rows of seats filled with familiar faces in disgusting blazers all staring at me. Something brushed against my fingers.

Someone was holding my hand.

It was Awful Agatha!

And when she realised that I realised that she was holding my hand, she pulled it away so fast she almost burned my fingers.

"So you're not dead then," she said. "Got any sandwiches?"

I rubbed my head. I was still groggy. My brain felt heavy and sloshed from side to side, like it was full of seawater.

"Big baby," Awful Agatha said.

"What?"

"If you go home, Sabzy, I'll have to annoy someone else."

I knew she was lying. But her lies were not as important as my lies. I couldn't be seen anywhere near an exhibition about my secret family.

"No, I have to go home," I said. "I'm still feeling dizzy and sick."

I grabbed my stomach, opened my mouth and did that throat-gagging thing to try and drag some vomit into my mouth.

Charlie scrambled to his feet. "Step back, everyone. She's gonna blow!"

The grown-ups leapt out of the way so fast they looked like they were doing the Hokey Cokey. I really am a brilliant actor. I could be an actor for a living. After all, I act out a fake character every day.

"No, it's ok, I think I can hold it," I said, standing up. "But if you can call Uncle Ernie, please, Miss Cannington, I really need to go home now."

"Ooh, yes, Uncle Ernie," said the Cannibal, in a really

high, giggly voice. "Yes, I remember your Uncle Ernie, such a handsome man."

Miss Shufflebottom and Mr Cumberlatch both stared at the headmistress.

"Such a handyman, I mean. He's such a handyman, isn't he, Sabrina? He's a very, *very* good handyman. Yes. So, er, Sabrina, how's your head?"

"Sore," I lied.

"Right, yes, I'll get your Uncle Handsome ... Handyman! ... Yes, your Uncle Handyman is a very good Ernie."

She almost ran out of the Planetarium.

Mr Cumberlatch tapped the watch on his wrist.

"It's almost time for our solar system show."

"Yeah, time for our solar system show," said Bonzo, tapping his wrist.

He didn't have a watch.

Mr Cumberlatch looked at Miss Shufflebottom and then pointed at me. She was so slow.

"Oh, yes, of course, come on Sabrina. We'll wait by the woolly mammoth for your uncle to arrive," she said. She put an arm around my shoulder and we staggered really slowly between the chairs. The Planetarium was so dark.

I heard the Cabbage Patch's voice over my shoulder.

"Ok, boys and girls, this show is twenty minutes long. There's no eating and no drinking. We don't want anyone dashing to the toilets. But there are toilets at the Royalty Exhibition, which is where we are heading to next."

The room wasn't spinning now, but my head was. I'd been

such a moron! Who cared if I went to the dumb exhibition or not? They'd still see pictures of me. Charlie already knew I was keeping a celebrity secret. He just thought I was a YouTube star. One photo on a wall would tell him everything. Awful Agatha, Liam, Miss Shufflebottom, they'd all know the truth, whether I was there or not. My fuzzy head had messed up my thinking. What was wrong with me? Awful Agatha was right. I had been a big baby, falling over and fainting. I needed to toughen up and smarten up. I needed a plan.

My job wasn't to keep ME away from the Princess Power display.

My job was to keep the WHOLE SCHOOL away from the Princess Power display.

"I want to stay," I said, in a voice that was probably way too loud.

"Are you sure?" Miss Shufflebottom asked.

"Is your head feeling better?" Charlie said.

"Give us a sandwich," said Awful Agatha.

"No, I'm fine now, really, let me stay, Miss Shufflebottom, please. I love planets and solar systems and the Milky Way and the way that stars collapse on themselves and form black holes."

Miss Shufflebottom looked into my eyes, like she was searching for something. It was totally awkward.

"Hmm, yes, I suppose so. But we'll have to monitor you. If you feel faint, then you have to let me know. And at some point, you'll have to tell me more about the science you did at your last school."

"Yes, Miss Shufflebottom. Thanks Miss Shufflebottom."

"All right, now go and find an available seat. The show is about to start. And I'll go and find Miss Cannington."

Thanks to my fainting, all the good seats were taken. Charlie was sitting with the boys who liked detective puzzles. Awful Agatha was sitting in an aisle seat, beside the teachers, because that's where Awful Agatha always had to sit.

It was hard to see in the dark, but I was pretty sure there was only one seat free.

Someone was patting the seat and waving at me. I squeezed past loads of legs and reached the last available seat.

Someone was still patting the seat.

"Can you move your hand please?" I asked.

"Sure."

I couldn't see his face, but I recognised the voice.

"I saved this seat just for you," said Liam.

Now I knew he had a crush on me. What a disaster.

Most people my age struggle with one crisis, but I had two. I had to keep the class away from the Royalty Exhibition and I had to keep love-struck Liam away from me.

But I was stuck inside a pitch-black planetarium. I was trapped.

CHAPTER FIVE

Liam kept trying to talk to me, but I had no time for his nonsense. He was going on and on about some bicycle kick he scored in a school football match, which sounded made up.

Maybe I wasn't listening. I was dealing with my own emergency. As soon as Mr Cumberlatch had stopped droning on about Jupiter and Saturn, the lights went down completely in the Planetarium. Once the place was totally dark, I sprang into action.

Uncle Ernie has always made me keep an emergency phone in my sock, for emergencies like this one.

My emergency phone was not a proper phone like normal children have, with apps and games and camera filters. It couldn't even make calls. In fact, I'm not even sure why I called the old-fashioned thing a phone. It was a small, rectangular black device with a tiny screen and a red button. All I had to do in emergencies was press the red button and Uncle Ernie would just appear, like a genie in a lamp, almost immediately.

It was so bizarre.

There was one time when Awful Agatha and me were in the local playground near my house and I was teaching her my unique fighting style of aikido and taekwondo, which I mixed together myself and was absolutely amazing.

And she accidentally booted me in the ankle, which didn't hurt because she kicked my emergency phone in my sock. She must have pushed the red button because minutes later, Uncle Ernie turned up, all out of breath and sweaty. He was still wearing his filthy white vest and pyjamas.

And, to really humiliate me, he came running around the corner, holding a hammer above his head and shouting "Aaarrrghhh!"

He looked like an escaped lunatic.

It was excruciating. Most children have uncles who take them for dinner or to the movies. My uncle runs around the local playground in his pyjamas, waving a hammer in the air and shouting "Aaarrrghhh!"

So I've been really careful with my emergency phone ever since.

But this was an emergency, the worst emergency since my country's stupid civil war forced me to leave my parents.

I needed a hero. I needed my Uncle Ernie.

"What are you doing down there?"

Liam was such a busybody, just like Charlie.

"Nothing," I lied, shoving my hand down my sock.

It was sweaty. I held my nose.

"The show is starting," Liam whispered.

"Watch it then."

"I want to watch it with you."

"Stop talking then."

"Did I tell you about my bicycle kick?"

"Yes."

"Oh. Shall I tell you about the hat-trick I scored last week?"

"No. I thought you wanted to watch the show."

"I do. Hey, I can burp the school song. I'm brilliant at burping."

"You're brilliant at not shutting up. Be quiet."

"Ssh!"

That was Miss Shufflebottom. If she came over, I'd be in a right pickle. She'd tell me to sit up and leave my sock alone, which would mean no emergency phone, no red button, no Uncle Ernie and no solution to my epic problem.

Finally I found the red button in the dark and pressed as hard as I could.

A red light flashed. Then the stupid thing beeped!

Everyone inside the Planetarium looked over at me.

So I started coughing, but tried to make each cough sound like a beep, which made me sound like a monkey with the hiccups. But my excellent acting worked. The rest of the class went back to watching the planets over our heads.

"What was that red light by your feet?" Liam asked.

"There wasn't a red light," I said, sitting up straight.

"Yes, there was. Hey, do you wear those soppy shoes for little kids? The ones that light up every time they step on the floor?"

"No."

Liam giggled.

"Yeah, you do. You wear those light-up shoes for babies."

I could make out his grinning, perfect teeth. I wanted to smash him right in the mouth. I had the perfect hook punch to do it, as well, but I had to keep a low profile. Besides, I knew that the Cabbage Patch was already suspicious.

"I can't believe you wear light-up shoes. That's so babyish."

"Yeah, you're right. I wear shoes that light up every time I step on the floor," I said.

"I knew it," Liam said, still spluttering all over his seat.

"Did I step on the floor?"

"What?"

"Did I step on the floor just now? Did I walk anywhere?"

"No."

"Then I'm not wearing light-up shoes, am I?"

"Well, what was it then?"

"I don't know, alright? Maybe a reflection from the planets."

"Ssh!"

Miss Shufflebottom's shushing was getting louder. She'd be over in a minute, with her finger on her lips.

Liam and me peered up at the top of the Planetarium. The show wasn't that bad actually. The different planets kept zooming in and out, spinning in front of our faces. Some of the dopey kids put their hands up, to block the planets. They thought the planets really were coming straight at them.

Through the corner of my eye, I saw Awful Agatha put her hands over her face and screamed when Mars popped out of the sky. The boys in front of her made fun of her so she booted the backs of their seats.

And then I felt woozy.

It wasn't the Planetarium show. It was something on my left hand. At first, I thought a spider had crawled across my fingers. Spiders don't bother me. I'm not afraid of insects or reptiles or any of the mammals that usually scare kids living in housing estates. In Mulakating, we had spiders, snakes and bats all around the Palace's forest and you shouldn't be scared of something if you see it all the time.

So I brushed the spider away and went back to watching Mercury soar over my head. But the spider came back. It crawled over my little finger, then the next finger, then another, and another and touched my thumb and stayed there.

The spider rested on my hand.

The spider covered my whole hand.

And then my brain started to work stuff out really quickly.

Spiders weren't that big in my new housing estate.

Spiders that were that big were usually much hairier, like tarantulas.

Spiders don't usually hang out in cold planetariums and sit on girls' hands.

If it wasn't a spider, then what else likes to hang out on a girl's hand?

It was another hand.

It was Liam's hand! It was a boy's hand!

Ew! That was gross. I thought I was going to throw up.

I felt so sick that I stopped thinking straight. My brain went to sleep and my body woke up. I turned into this robot, but a really weird robot that happens to be superb at aikido. It was like being in a dream while I was still awake.

In the darkness, I watched my right hand grab Liam's wrist and yank his arm into the air. He made this yelping sound, like a puppy dog, but I didn't stop. I was in the zone. I was the aikido robot defending myself.

My left hand grabbed his right elbow and twisted, which pulled his whole body out of his seat and sent him spinning towards the floor.

He landed on his knees and was still make that yelping noise. So now, he sounded and looked like a puppy dog. But the aikido move wasn't finished. I pinned his arm against his back, just like the cops on those TV dramas do when they arrest suspects and slap on the handcuffs. But I didn't need a cop's handcuffs. I had Uncle Ernie's aikido lessons.

I pushed Liam's arm along his spine until his hand was almost touching the back of his neck.

"Ah, my arm, my arm," he squealed. "You're breaking my arm, Sabrina!"

At that exact moment the show stopped and the Planetarium lights came on.

Liam was still on his knees, squeezed between two rows of seats. I was still standing over Liam and still holding his wrist, like I was in a trance.

"The lights are on," he whimpered. "Will you please let go off my arm?"

I snapped out of my aikido zone, dropped his arm and jumped back.

"Ow," he cried.

"Oh, I'm so sorry, Liam," I said. "I didn't mean to ... It's just that ..."

I had forgotten how to make sentences. I had forgotten

how to do anything. I just stood there, in the middle of the Planetarium, watching everyone watch me.

Miss Shufflebottom covered her mouth. Charlie rubbed his eyes. Awful Agatha gave me a big thumbs up.

"Nice one, Sabzy," she cheered.

That wasn't helpful.

And then I saw the bony finger of Mr Cumberlatch pointed at me.

"Well, young lady," he said. "I think it's time you left my Planetarium. Now!"

CHAPTER SIX

The four adults surrounded me, taking turns to tell me off. Well, there were three adults and Bonzo. He wasn't really an adult. He was just a Bonzo.

Mr Cumberlatch did most of the talking, more than the teachers, which sort of made sense, as it was his beloved Planetarium.

"Screenings at our Planetarium are very expensive, young lady," he said.

"Yeah, very expensive," said Bonzo.

"We must reset the projector for each screening."

"Yeah, projector, must reset it."

"And school parties and tour groups are on fixed schedules."

"Yeah, school parties, fixed schedules."

"My time is too important for you to monkey around."

"Yeah, his time is too important. He's a monkey."

"Will you be quiet, Bonzo!"

The Cabbage Patch looked like he was going to whack Bonzo, who ducked out of the way. Bonzo was already hunched over and swayed from side to side like an orangutan. He also had floppy, ginger hair and long arms, which made him look even more like an orangutan. He probably went home and slept in a tree every night.

But even Bonzo didn't seem as nervous as his boss. Sweat

trickled down the Cabbage Patch's long nose, like a snowball on a ski slope.

"I don't know what to do about this," he said. "I need to continue the tour. But you've already fainted at the entrance and got into a fight in the Planetarium. What are you going to do in our Royalty Exhibition? Set the place on fire?"

That didn't seem like a bad idea.

There were actually two reasons why I was utterly desperate not to set foot in that ridiculous exhibition. The first one was obvious: My class couldn't know the truth about my family.

But the second reason turned my stomach. It was the real reason why I fainted.

I didn't want to see their faces.

My parents.

Up close.

I didn't want to see them smiling back at me, like they used to every morning at breakfast and every night at bedtime when we drank hot chocolate with marshmallows.

I didn't want to see their faces. Not today.

I wouldn't faint. I wouldn't panic. I wouldn't even get scared.

But my heart would shatter into a million pieces.

"Maybe I can explain, Mr Cumberlatch." Miss Cannington had decided to speak on my behalf. At the Palace, grown-ups often spoke on my behalf, so I didn't mind.

"Explain what?"

The Cabbage Patch was running out of patience.

"Yeah, explain what?"

"Bonzo, would you please stop repeating my words."

"Yes, boss. I'll stop repeating your words."

"Bonzo, look, why don't you go ahead to the Royalty Exhibition and check everything is ready for the class?"

"Yes, boss."

The hallway was starting to spin again. Bonzo became a blur as he hurried off towards the Princess Power nonsense, where there were going to be photographs of my family and photographs of *me*.

I just *knew* it.

"As I was saying, Mr Cumberlatch, Sabrina hasn't been at our school very long and it's been a difficult period of adjustment."

No, it hadn't. My headmistress was telling a blatant lie. Moving to a rubbish school in the middle of nowhere didn't need a *period of adjustment*, as she called it, using her teacher vocabulary. Leaving my home because there was a civil war and half the country wanted to stick my family in prison, that was the *period of adjustment*, you daft old cannibal.

"Yes, she's usually such a sweet and kind young girl." Miss Shufflebottom had suddenly remembered how to speak.

"A very sweet and kind young girl," the Cannibal added.

Now they were repeating each other.

The Cabbage Patch hummed really loudly, trying to work out what to do with me.

"Yes, but we have a strict policy at our museum when it comes to fighting. It should be an automatic exclusion."

"I was feeling giddy!" I had finally found my voice. I was just waiting for my brain to catch up.

"What?"

"Yeah, I fainted, remember? I was barely conscious. I couldn't focus on my surroundings."

Mr Cumberlatch seemed suspicious.

"She speaks very well, doesn't she?"

"Oh, yes. We're very proud of our students," the Cannibal beamed. "It's not just vocabulary, but pronunciation, enunciation and a deep respect for the communicative process."

"GIVE ME A SANDWICH OR I'LL PUNCH YOU RIGHT UP THE EAR!"

Awful Agatha's booming voice came through the Planetarium curtain. Our headmistress blushed.

"Miss Shufflebottom, could you have a word with Agatha? And please tell her it's 'in' not 'up'. She's going to punch someone 'right *in* the ear', not '*up* the ear'."

The Cabbage Patch looked horrified.

"No, she's not going to punch anyone in your museum," said the old Cannibal. "I just cannot tolerant poor grammar."

But she grabbed Miss Shufflebottom and whispered in her ear.

"Make sure Agatha doesn't punch anyone, until we're back on the school bus."

And then she returned to me.

"What were you saying, Sabrina?"

"Yes, well, I was feeling a little delirious when I felt

something on my hand, in the dark. I thought it was a spider."

The Cabbage Patch bit his bottom lip. "I can assure you, young lady, that there are no insects in my museum, unless they are dead and stuffed and inside a glass case. We have this place fogged and fumigated regularly. There are no insects here!"

"Isn't a spider an arachnid, not an insect?"

I probably shouldn't have said that. The Cabbage Patch looked like his face was melting.

"Never mind insects and arachnids," he said. "I saw your shenanigans. You grabbed that boy's wrist, flipped him like a pancake and almost tore his arm off! How many spiders feel like a boy's hand?"

"I thought it was a big spider."

The Cabbage Patch took a step towards me. He switched on his torch and shined it right in my face. My eyes started watering, but I wasn't scared. Bullies don't bother me.

"Hmm, that sounded like sarcasm," he said. "And you suddenly look so familiar to me."

The torch's giant circle of light made me blink away the tears. I felt like I was being interrogated at a police station. But I wouldn't crack under pressure.

"I really don't think that's possible, Mr Cumberlatch. She hasn't lived in the area for very long," said Miss Cannington.

The bright glare covered my entire face. I could feel my cheeks getting warmer. The tall, skinny museum guide leaned over so far he looked like a giraffe drinking water from a lake. I thought his back might snap.

"Your face. Where have I seen your face?"

He was so close I could see those long curly hairs up his nostrils. He really should ask for a nose trimmer for his next birthday.

"It's coming to me. That face. I've seen you before, right here, in the museum. I know I have. Oh yes. Maybe that's it. I think I've seen you at the ..."

"URGENT CALL FOR YOU, SIR!"

A security guard grabbed his arm.

"You've got a call in the office," said the security guard.

The Cabbage Patch ignored the security guard.

"Wait, I'm trying to remember where I've seen this girl before."

"It's urgent, sir, this way please, sir."

The security guard pulled Cabbage Patch's elbow.

"Yes, all right, all right. There's no need to touch me. I know where my office is, thank you very much."

The Cabbage Patch switched off his torch and straightened his revolting lime green jacket. I nearly laughed as he fixed his tie. He looked like a praying mantis.

"Give the kids a toilet break and then I'll take them to the Royalty Exhibition."

He dashed through the Planetarium curtain. Maybe he needed a toilet break.

The security guard had interrupted at the right moment. I could've kissed him. Even though he had a scruffy beard and funny glasses, I still could've kissed him because I knew who he really was.

CHAPTER SEVEN

Miss Cannington really likes my Uncle Ernie, in that irritating way when grown-ups act like children. At school, she's always making excuses to talk to him, which are so obvious to anyone with half a brain. She calls me over in the playground and makes these childish requests.

Hey Sabrina, our next unit of enquiry is arts and craft. Why not invite your Uncle Ernie to give a talk because he's a handyman, right?

Hey Sabrina, maybe we need a parent-teacher conference with your Uncle Ernie?

Hey Sabrina, has anyone ever said that your Uncle Ernie looks like George Clooney?

The old Cannibal has been obsessed with Uncle Ernie since the first time they met. To me, he's old, grey, slightly senile and produces too many bad smells that he blames on the gas.

But he always does this strange thing: When he tells a rubbish joke, women laugh at him, like a proper belly laugh, like the kind of belly laugh I had when he tripped over my shoes on the doorstep and head-butted the dustbin. My mother said Uncle Ernie always made women go weak at the knees, which sounded ridiculous to me. I don't want any boy to make me go weak at the knees.

I'd fall over.

Uncle Ernie makes me cringe. He's not handsome or funny. He's just my Uncle Ernie and, to be honest, I don't like the idea of sharing him with anyone.

He's family.

He's my only family at the moment.

So the last thing I needed was Miss Cannington's flirting. Plus, I couldn't have her asking awkward questions, things like: "Oh, hello, Mr Parslowe. I didn't expect to see you dressed as a security guard at the museum. Why are you wearing a fake beard and funny glasses?"

As she examined Uncle Ernie's eyes, I felt like I'd been kicked in the guts. I mean, it was so ridiculously obvious that he was wearing a stuck-on beard and glasses that were far too big for his head.

I waited for the latest crisis to hit my lousy day.

"Oh hello," I heard her say. "You look awfully familiar. My name's Miss Cannington. And you are?"

I couldn't believe what I was seeing. She was holding out her hand to shake. She had no clue. She was as blind as a blindfolded bat locked in a dark cupboard.

"I'm Sammy. I'm the museum security guard," said Uncle Ernie. "I'm Sammy the security guard."

I rolled my eyes.

"Really? That's your name?"

"Sabrina, don't be rude."

"No, it's fine, Miss Cannington. Yes, I really am Sammy the security guard. See?"

Uncle Ernie tapped a nameplate that was pinned to his uniform. It literally said, "Sammy the Security Guard."

Miss Cannington kept peering into Uncle Ernie's bright, blue eyes. "I must have seen you here on our previous museum trip, last year?"

Uncle Ernie ran a hand through his grey hair and smiled. Now the old Cannibal looked like she was going to faint. She seemed all weak and wobbly.

"Nah, I've just got one of those faces," said Uncle Ernie. "But I've definitely seen your face before. You're an actress, right?"

The old Cannibal jiggled around like her bladder was about to burst. Her fluttering eyelashes looked like butterfly wings.

"Ooh, Sammy, you're making me blush. I'm not an actress. Well, that's not strictly true. I did once appear in our local drama society's production of *The Lion, the Witch and the Wardrobe*."

"You didn't play the witch surely."

"No, I played the wardrobe."

I felt something tickle the back of my throat. Even Uncle Ernie coughed. How we didn't laugh like a couple of hyenas I will never know.

"I'm sure you were an excellent wardrobe."

"I was very tall and could stand still for a long time."

"Well, I'd certainly watch you playing a wardrobe, Miss Cannington."

Now I felt sick at the back of my throat.

"Do you mind if I have a quick word with this young lady?

I promised Mr Cumberlatch I would just go over the rules and regulations of the museum."

The old Cannibal frowned. I could tell she needed to be convinced to leave.

"Miss Cannington, I think I just heard Agatha stealing Charlie's sandwiches."

"Oh, not again," she muttered. "Ok, two minutes and then I'll meet you beside the toilets outside the Royalty Exhibition. Excuse me, Sammy ... AGATHA!"

She pulled back the curtain to the Planetarium and vanished.

Uncle Ernie dragged me to a darkened corner, away from the exit.

"It's me," he whispered.

"I know."

"No, not Sammy the Security Guard, it's me," he said again, lifting his glasses.

"I know it's you."

"Uncle Ernie."

"I know!"

He looked disappointed.

"How did you see through my brilliant disguise?"

"It's not a brilliant disguise, is it?"

"The fake beard was good."

"I'm having the worst day ever, Uncle Ernie. Stop talking about your beard."

"But I even got a beard that matches my grey hair. See?"

He pulled the beard off and put it on top of his head. He

was right. The hair colour was a perfect match.

"Ok, fine. It's the best beard ever. How did you get here so fast? And where did you get the uniform from?"

"Oh it was just something I had lying around in my wardrobe."

"Yeah, right. A security guard's uniform for the museum I'm visiting today?"

"I have an unusual taste in fashion. Now pay attention, Sabrina."

And he told me everything. Well, almost everything. Ever since we were forced to leave the Palace, Uncle Ernie and I had become world champion liars. We lie so often that we rarely remember when we're telling the truth. Plus, I don't think Uncle Ernie has ever told the truth in his entire life. He calls himself a handyman, but I've never seen him put up a shelf or fix a broken TV, yet I have seen him karate chop a thief in Mulakating. Handymen don't do that, do they?

He had followed me to the museum, where he had heard Mr Cumberlatch tell me off outside the Planetarium.

"I have to say, Sabrina. I didn't like what I was hearing," he said.

"Yeah, I know. Sorry about using my aikido on Liam."

"No, I'm talking about that dreadful Cumberlatch man giving you a lecture. I'm thinking about giving him a karate chop outside the Royalty Exhibition."

"You can't do that!"

"No, you're right. Too many witnesses. I'll give him a karate chop in the toilets."

"There will be no karate chopping, Uncle Ernie. How are we going to keep the class away from the Royalty Exhibition? Have you seen it yet?"

Uncle Ernie's face went all funny, but not in a funny way. He looked deadly serious. Maybe it was the dark corridor outside the Planetarium, but I'm sure his eyes went watery.

"Yeah, I saw them," he said, really softly.

"Them?"

"Your mum and dad. There are photos of them."

Now I was the one being karate chopped in the stomach. When I thought about their faces, I saw their beautiful, sparkly smiles and that always sets me off.

I couldn't be a blubbing wreck, not today.

But they were still my Mummy and Daddy. And I still, you know, the L-word, both of them, all the time, every minute of every day and especially at night, when I was alone in bed and could think about them as much as I wanted and no one could stop me. If my eyes leaked, then so what? I was alone. I was always alone. That's why my eyes leaked!

Part of me really wanted to see them, even if they were just photographs in a dusty old museum.

"What do they look like?"

Uncle Ernie spluttered a bit. He was having trouble speaking.

"They look young. It's an old photo, taken from their wedding day, which is good for us, in a way. They don't really look like that anymore."

"I can't see them. I know I can't, but I really want to, even if it's really quick, just for a second, in the photograph. Does that sound silly?" Now I knew I had tears in my eyes.

"No, of course it's not silly."

Uncle Ernie stretched out his arms.

"What are you doing?" I said. "Are you putting your arms around me? Don't put your arms around me. You can't hug me, not here."

"Sorry."

I felt bad. Sometimes I think that I'm the only one in the world to have lost people, but Uncle Ernie had lost his best friends.

"It's all right, Uncle Ernie. So ... er ... what does the photo of me look like?"

"There isn't one."

"What?"

"There are no photos of you in the exhibition."

"None at all?"

Suddenly, I was jumping up and down and grabbing Uncle Ernie's fake uniform.

"That's the best news ever. Why didn't you tell me before? If there are no photos of me and just an old one of my parents then we should be fine, right? Right?"

I was still jumping and down. But Uncle Ernie wasn't.

Why wasn't he excited?

He put his hands on my shoulders to stop me hopping like a lunatic.

"Not quite," he said. "The Princess Power part of the exhibition is the real problem. You have no photos there. But you do have a life-sized waxwork figure."

CHAPTER EIGHT

Now I had to deal with two of me in the Mayesbrook Museum of Modern and Ancient Wonders. There was the real me, which I had to keep away from that suspicious Mr Cumberlatch with the ski-slope nose. And there was the fake waxwork me that I had to keep away from every single person on the school trip.

Uncle Ernie sent me packing back to the group, before they got worried. He went off to come up with one of his cunning plans, which were usually not very cunning.

But secretly, I was glad that he was here, in the museum, keeping an eye on me. He's always kept an eye on me, ever since I was a baby at the Palace. He's the only person I completely trust, the only person I have with me from the Palace.

I'd be lost without Uncle Ernie.

I'd have no one.

But I couldn't think about that now.

I ran past the Planetarium, along the darkened corridors, which are always too long in museums. I know they are full of paintings and historical facts, but let's be honest. Most of us want to get to the interactive bits, things we can touch, press, draw and bang. But the long corridor gave me a chance to think clearly. I knew I was going to get bombarded with questions from everyone. I had to be prepared.

Miss Cannington, Miss Shufflebottom and a red-faced Liam were waiting for me outside the toilets.

The old Cannibal went first.

"What did the security guard say?"

"He said that there should be no more fighting in the museum and I promised to be on my best behaviour for the rest of the day."

"Yes, no more fighting," Miss Shufflebottom said.

"But we weren't fighting, Miss!"

Liam sounded really angry, but looked down at his shoes. He was so embarrassed. That's the funny thing about the boys in my class. When they are embarrassed, they get angry, which only makes them more embarrassed and it goes round and round in circles until they go crazy.

"Please don't raise your voice, Liam," Miss Shufflebottom said.

"But we didn't fight, did we?"

And then Liam looked straight at me! He flicked his hair away from his face. His eyes were popping out of his head like a cartoon character.

"Tell them that we didn't have a fight. Tell them."

For a moment, I thought Liam's eyes might spring a leak. Princesses are not supposed to cry, but I know for an absolute fact that boys definitely can't, not at our age and certainly not on a school trip.

It was so obvious what had happened.

I bet Liam's friends had wondered how a girl had thrown him to the floor with her spectacular aikido moves, which seems really sexist to me. But some boys still believe that they are better than girls, which is so ironic because those boys are usually the weakest boys around.

Liam couldn't admit he'd been done over by a girl, not at our school, not with people like Awful Agatha around to remind him every five minutes. But he couldn't say that nothing had happened either. When the lights came on inside the Planetarium, I had him pinned to the floor. He was literally on his knees and screaming like a baby. He didn't look cool, did he?

I had to come up with a clever explanation, but I wanted to see if his story was better than mine first.

"No, we didn't have a fight," I said. "Tell them what really happened, Liam."

He sniffed and wiped his nose on his grotty green blazer.

"Yeah, what happened was, Sabrina said she couldn't see the show. The seats in front were blocking her. So I said she could sit on my back."

Liam was an idiot.

And then he smiled at me, as if he'd just solved the greatest mystery in the universe. He was almost handsome when he smiled. Almost. No boys are handsome when they smile, except my father, but he was an exception.

Liam had dimples in his cheeks. But he also had a dopey brain. He was a bit of a dopey dimple.

The old Cannibal was frowning. Her hands were stuck on her hips. She knew the story was a load of rubbish, too.

"Why would Sabrina sit on your back, Liam?"

"To see over the seat in front, Miss Cannington."

"But she's taller than you."

"Oh yeah. But, you know, sometimes, when you get a big head in front of you, you know like a big basketball head, you can't always see the screen."

"But it was the Planetarium. The screen was above your head, on the ceiling."

"Oh yeah. Right. Well, she thought my back was a pillow!"

"What?"

I had to save the fool. He was making us both look ridiculous.

"It's ok, Liam, I'll tell the truth. You don't have to protect me."

"Don't I?"

He had no idea what was going on.

"He doesn't want to get me into trouble because we weren't allowed to eat in the Planetarium and I asked him to get a sandwich from my bag. So he got down on his hands and knees in the dark."

The old Cannibal suddenly had loads of squiggly lines on her forehead.

"Is that really what happened, Sabrina?

"Yeah, is that what happened, Sabrina?" Liam wondered.

I gave him a dirty look. He didn't know when to shut up.

"Yes, Miss Cannington. But he couldn't find the sandwich in my bag so I leaned over, but I couldn't see in the dark and fell on top of him, which made him jump. I grabbed his arm to pull him up and that's when the light came on."

"Yeah, that's when the light came on," Liam said, the light finally coming on in his brain. "That's exactly what happened, Miss, the sandwich in the bag, and the falling and stuff."

I nodded loads of times, to show how much I agreed with our made-up story.

"I know I shouldn't have eaten inside the Planetarium, but I was hungry after fainting. It won't happen again, Miss Cannington."

Miss Shufflebottom seemed satisfied, but she always was. The old Cannibal wasn't entirely convinced, but I knew my lie had given her a convenient explanation and she was more worried about our museum itinerary.

"Ok, well, as long as you're not feeling weak anymore," she said.

"No, I'm fine now, Miss Cannington."

"Hmm, ok, and Liam, I know it's easier sometimes to make up stories, but in the end, they just make life more complicated."

For once, I agreed with her. No one's life was more complicated than mine.

The teachers marched off to deal with Awful Agatha, who was chasing the boys with her water bottle and shouting the lyrics to "Singin' in the Rain".

Liam stared at his shoes again.

"Thanks for doing that."

"It's all right."

"Didn't you like me holding your hand in the Planetarium?"

"No."

"Can I hold your hand later?"

"No."

"What about when we go to the Princess Power thing ... what's wrong?"

What was wrong? Everything was wrong. Liam might be a dopey with dimples, but even he could see that I was a bag of nerves. Making up a brilliant cover story for my aikido had at least made me forget about the real disaster.

"Nothing's wrong. Leave me alone."

I needed time to think, but of course I didn't get any because my actual friends turned up and demanded to know what I'd been doing.

"Why do you keep hanging out with Liam?" Charlie asked.

"I'm not. He keeps following me around. Like you."

Poor Charlie looked ready to burst into tears.

"I thought you like being with me."

"I do. It's just that I have a much bigger problem right now."

"I just poured my water bottle on that boy's head."

"That's great, Agatha."

"I'm gonna pour water on Liam's head."

"No, wait."

I grabbed Awful Agatha's arm, which made her shriek at me. Agatha does not like to be touched. Ever.

I stepped back from her, which made me stomp on Charlie's tiny toes. So he screamed at me.

Everyone was screaming. So I couldn't do any thinking. Luckily, a voice silenced Charlie and Awful Agatha, but it was the wrong voice.

"I can't speak while everyone is talking."

In the dark corridor outside the toilets, Mr Cumberlatch and Bonzo stepped into the light. The Cabbage Patch was sweating and clearly stressed.

"Right, that's enough time spent on naughty children and phantom security guards," he said, looking at me the whole time.

"There will be no more delays, no more distractions. We are going to the Royalty Exhibition to see the Princess Power waxwork figures right now."

CHAPTER NINE

Mr Cumberlatch was making us walk really fast. Too fast. He was practically running. My head was soft and squishy like scrambled eggs. I kept hearing the Cabbage Patch's words, over and over again, like a YouTube clip repeating itself.

The museum is a spider's web.

The museum's map looks like a spider's web.

Every long corridor led back to the middle, back to that lame Royalty Exhibition, the one with the Princess Power display, the one with a waxwork figure of me.

What sort of name was that anyway?

Princess Power.

Princesses don't have any power. Duh.

If they had power they wouldn't be princesses, would they? Kings and queens had power. Or they did in the old days until all that power went to politicians, and kings and queens became people who just waved at strangers.

But I knew what the museum was doing. I wasn't born yesterday. Princesses are old-fashioned and girly and wear frilly dresses. And now, young women were independent and strong and wore whatever they wanted, but I had always been independent and strong and wore whatever I wanted—except on days when I had to wave at strangers.

So this museum thought it was doing me a huge favour,

when it was doing the exact opposite. If that waxwork figure revealed my secret, then I would be finished. And maybe my parents would be finished. And I wasn't going to let that happen.

I was the princess with power, not some waxwork that probably looked nothing like me. My parents took me to the Mulakating Museum of Wax once and we had to pretend we were impressed with the place because we were special guests. But none of the wax figures looked real. They looked like skinny white candles.

They looked like Mr Cumberlatch.

"Come along now, children, once we get around this corner, we'll be at the Royalty Exhibition," he said. "All our royals are made with lots of wax."

"Yeah, all our royals are made with lots of tax."

"Not tax, Bonzo. Wax!"

Bonzo giggled as he tried to keep up with his boss. His arms dangled at his sides. His hands were so low that his knuckles almost scraped against the marble floor. The Cabbage Patch's lanky legs made him move like a flamingo. I stayed at the back of the group, shuffling along as slowly as possible. I was hoping for a genius idea to smack me in the brain. But nothing was happening.

Charlie and Awful Agatha walked beside me because Charlie always walked beside me, whether I was slow or fast, and Awful Agatha preferred to hide at the back just to annoy the teachers.

I wiped my forehead. The sweat rolled through my hair.

"What's wrong with you?" Charlie said.

"I don't want to go into this exhibition."

"Yeah, nor do I," Awful Agatha said. "Who wants to see Princess Power? It sounds like the worst movie ever."

"It's not a movie. It's an exhibition. It's like a collection of historical stuff."

"Are you making fun of me, Charlie?"

"No, of course not, Agatha."

"Because if you are I'll boot you right in the—"

"Be quiet. I'm trying to concentrate."

Awful Agatha wasn't scared of anyone, except maybe her parents and she didn't like talking about them. But even she stopped talking. She knew I was worried about something.

We turned the corner and there it was. The words were written above the enormous marble archway: ROYALTY EXHIBITION.

Even from a distance, the exhibition seemed huge, like an airport terminal. People were dashing around everywhere, taking photos of massive paintings in golden frames and posing in front of old costumes. At the back of the grand hall, a long way away, there was a collection of models in glittery dresses.

Waxwork figures.

Princesses.

Princess Sabrina Valence of Mulakating, the daughter of King Halbutt and Queen Beverly from the House of Valence, was waiting for me.

I was about to see myself covered in wax. My friends were

going to see their secretive classmate dressed as a princess inside a museum.

My limbs were shaking. Everything was wobbling in slow motion. My eyes were stinging. I took loads of deep breaths and started mumbling to myself.

You will not faint again.

You will not faint again.

You will not faint again.

"I think she's not feeling well," Charlie said.

"I think she's a nutter," Awful Agatha said. "She's probably hungry. Have a sandwich. And give me one as well."

"I can't go in there. I can't go in there," I said, over and over again.

Charlie stood on tiptoes and whispered into my ear.

"Do you think people will recognise you in there?"

"Yes, yes, I'll definitely get recognised in there."

"Just stand behind me then. I'll shield you."

"Charlie, you're shorter than me."

Charlie couldn't help me. Awful Agatha certainly couldn't help me. She couldn't help herself half the time. We were heading to the Royalty Exhibition. The Cabbage Patch and Bonzo were almost at the arched entrance.

I had no plan, no escape route, no brilliant idea, nothing. Uncle Ernie always called me his Princess Incognito.

I was seconds away from no longer being incognito.

And then, I stumbled into a fog.

The air turned cloudy and grey. My eyes were burning. I felt like I'd fallen into a fire. Something was scratching the back of my throat. I was coughing. I heard Charlie and Awful Agatha coughing. Everyone was coughing.

We had all disappeared into a mysterious fog. Everyone had vanished. We were just voices, coughing voices.

"It's all gassy and smelly," I heard Charlie say.

"Have you farted, Charlie?"

"No, I haven't, Agatha."

"You did just now, outside the toilets."

"That was you."

"Oh, yeah. Well, it's not my fault. It's the cheese."

"Ladies and gentlemen, there's no need to panic. Everybody stay calm."

It was a man's voice, but not Mr Cumberlatch's voice. And it wasn't Bonzo's voice because he was a man-child, or an ape-child really.

Through the fog, an astronaut appeared, or some sort of spaceman anyway. Maybe he was a fake alien, from the Future Earth exhibition. He wore a baggy, brown uniform and a mask that covered his entire head.

He was definitely an astronaut, or an alien. He wasn't human anyway.

He raised his arms through the fog. He was holding something long, pointy and silver.

A GUN!

It was definitely a gun, or some sort of intergalactic weapon.

We put our hands in the air and surrendered.

"No, no, no, everything is fine, boys and girls," the

astronaut or alien said. "I'm John Johnson from John Johnson Pest Control. You find the pest, we do the rest, because we're the best. We just got a call that this exhibition is full of the Norwegian Death Clock Beetle. So we are fumigating."

The fog slowly cleared so Mr Cumberlatch, who was still coughing a lot, waved the clouds away and marched over to the pest controller.

"Now, I've had just about enough of this."

The Cabbage Patch stood so close to the pest controller that his nose almost touched John Johnson's mask.

"Now, look here. Argh!"

John Johnson fogged Mr Cumberlatch's face.

"Oh, I'm so sorry about that. This fogging spray gun has a mind of its own. But not to worry, it's harmless to humans. But you should see what it does to a Norwegian Death Clock Beetle. First, it melts its brain. Then it makes the eyes pop. Then the beetle's bottom falls off."

Miss Cannington waved her hands in front of the pest controller's face.

"Yes, yes, we don't need a pest control commentary. What do we do now?"

"Go to the next exhibition. I'll be done in half an hour and you can come back."

"And in the other exhibitions, are there any, you know, Norwegian dead baby rattle thingies?"

"No, you're completely fine. Off you go."

The pest controller lead us away from his foggy entrance.

Mr Cumberlatch was already standing at the back with Bonzo, moaning about the lack of communication in his museum.

The teachers told us to gather around Miss Shufflebottom's map to decide where to go next. That should've been the Cabbage Patch's job, but he was still sulking about being fogged in the face.

The students were already arguing over which exhibition to visit. I couldn't care less. I was thinking only about my exit.

"Hey."

It wasn't Charlie or Awful Agatha. They were bickering as usual. Charlie wanted to go to the Future Earth exhibition for the interactive puzzles. Awful Agatha preferred the Chamber of Nightmares because she wanted to terrify everyone.

"Behind you."

The pest controller tapped me on the shoulder.

"Hello, Sabrina."

"Hello, Uncle Ernie."

We spoke slyly, through the sides of our mouths, like secret agents in spy movies.

"How did you know it was me?"

"There's no such thing as a Norwegian Death Clock Beetle."

"I know. Funny right?"

Uncle Ernie actually giggled behind his mask, right in the middle of our crisis. He lifted his gun sprayer thing and fogged the air around us. I couldn't see a thing.

"Are you trying to kill me?"

"It's camouflage. No one can see us talking. Anyway, this fogging spray is harmless. There are no side effects."

"Really?"

"Sure. You wouldn't mind if your hair fell out, right?"

"What?"

"I'm kidding. Listen. I've bought you some time. So give me some time to work out a plan for your waxwork figure. Oh, and you have one more problem."

"I don't want any more problems!"

"It's over there."

Even through the fog, I spotted what Uncle Ernie was nodding at. Behind our group, Mr Cumberlatch was muttering something to Bonzo. He kept looking round to make sure no one else was listening, so it was obviously top-secret information.

"What's going on, Uncle Ernie?"

"When I was in Mulakating, I was taught to lip-read."

"Why would a handyman need to lip-read?"

"It's hard to hear other handymen on noisy building sites."

"Yeah, right."

"Anyway, I saw what the skinny one said to the daft one."

Uncle Ernie fogged the air one more time. I couldn't see his hand, but felt it brush against my shoulder. He wanted to give me a hug. My stomach turned into mushy peas. I wanted to hug him too, but I had to pretend I didn't even know him.

"You need to be really careful now," said Uncle Ernie.

"Why?"

"The tall one thinks he recognises you. He keeps seeing you speaking to the staff. He thinks you are hiding something. He's making Bonzo his spy. So wherever you go, Bonzo will be spying on you."

CHAPTER TEN

Uncle Ernie said we only had two jobs for the day. He had to take care of my life-sized waxwork figure. And I had to keep everyone away from the Royalty Exhibition.

Easy peasy lemon squeezy.

And yes, that was sarcasm.

Most kids my age worry about their maths homework (Charlie) or how many goals they score (Liam) or how many sandwiches they eat (Awful Agatha). And they really stress over this stuff, too. Charlie thinks it's the end of the world if he can't answer one of his detective maths puzzles. Liam has to believe that he's the greatest footballer in the school or he sulks. And if Awful Agatha gets too hungry, she punches someone.

But they're not real problems, are they? Not really. Not like mine. And I know that everyone says that. Everyone thinks their problems are the worst in the world because they are *their* problems. But does any other 11-year-old seriously have to put up with my daily disasters? And I was on my own. Uncle Ernie had already legged it, spraying visitors with his fogging gun.

Luckily, Mr Cumberlatch had led us to the Future Earth exhibition. There were loads of interactive artworks on the wall, for kids to touch and move around, which meant the gallery had to be quite dark, which was fantastic news for me.

I could sneak around in the darkness.

The Cabbage Patch was standing at the front of this massive screen that covered the entire wall. It was bigger than a cinema screen. Lots of drawings moved around behind his head.

"This exhibition is called 'Our City'," he said.

"That doesn't look like our city," said Awful Agatha.

"No, it's a fake city."

"Then it's not our city then, is it?"

"Agatha! That's enough," said Miss Cannington.

The Cabbage Patch pointed at the glowing screen.

"Ah, but it is your city. Look carefully. Children like you drew these pictures of themselves and then they scanned them in that machine over there and the pictures came alive on this wall behind me."

He gave us a demonstration of what we had to do. He made us stand around him at a table with loads of pencils and pieces of paper, which was terrible for the environment. He drew a round face, which looked nothing like him.

He was rubbish at drawing.

"I can't tell if that's a man or a woman. Draw the other bits."

The Cabbage Patch ignored Awful Agatha's childish joke and shoved his drawing into a dark black machine that lit up.

When he took the paper back out, he said, "Now, this is 2D."

"No, it's a piece of paper," said Awful Agatha.

The Cabbage Patch rolled his eyes. "The drawing of my face was 2D, which means it's flat. Now, look at the screen."

We waited for a few seconds and then his round face appeared on the screen. It was walking! His round face had been stuck on to a different body. His body was wearing a suit. And his drawing walked around with other drawings. They wore suits and dresses and all kinds of random clothes. Some were nurses and doctors and teachers and firemen and cleaners. The drawings of all the heads were on different bodies and walking along streets and past buildings. The students oohed and aahed and all that sort of stuff. Even Awful Agatha stopped talking. The 'Our City' thing was unusual, but really cool.

"My 2D drawing of my face has turned into a 3D drawing. It's no longer a flat face. It's a fully-rounded head and walking around with other fully-rounded drawings. This teaches us urban planning and city design and ..."

No one was listening anymore. They were pushing each other to get a seat and fighting over the pencils.

I waited. I was in no rush. The place was gloomy, my friends were distracted and there were no waxwork figures of me. I wanted to stay in Future Earth all day.

"Draw something."

I turned around. Bonzo was standing right behind me. He had been spying on me the whole time!

I felt my hands turning into fists. I had so many brilliant aikido and taekwondo moves. I could flip him. Kick him. Punch him. Spin him. Anything.

But I had to stay calm. There is such a thing called princess etiquette. It's a fancy way of saying posh behaviour. Princesses have to speak and stand in a certain way, shake hands in a certain way and treat people in a certain way. And I'm pretty sure that princesses can't kick silly boys called Bonzo in his private parts.

"Are you following me?"

"Er, no, no, I'm not following you, hur hur. I'm looking at this."

Bonzo turned and pointed at an empty wall.

"There's nothing there. It's just blank," I said.

"I like blank. I'm a bit blank, hur hur!"

"You are following me."

"I'm not."

"You're standing right behind me."

"I'm not ... oh yeah, I am standing right behind you, hur hur."

"Why are you standing right behind me?"

"Er, well, when we have school groups, Mr Cumberlatch stands at the front and I stand at the back, so we don't lose anyone. Yeah. That's it. We never, ever lose anyone on our school tours."

Miss Shufflebottom came over.

"I think we've lost Agatha," she said.

I was desperate to laugh. But mostly, I was actually pleased to see Miss Shufflebottom.

"Have you guys seen her?"

Bonzo scratched his head. "Which one is Agatha?"

"She's the tall girl, the one we've been calling Agatha all morning."

"She's probably gone to the toilet, Miss Shufflebottom. She does that sometimes, when we have group activities."

"Yes, she does, doesn't she? You really are a smart girl, aren't you, Sabrina?"

"Not really. I just say what I see." I looked straight at Bonzo. "Well, you sit with the others and draw your face and I'll go and get Agatha."

She hurried towards the exit.

"Miss Shufflebottom," I shouted after her. "When Agatha thinks she's not good at something, when she's not as good as the rest of us, she goes a bit, well ..."

Miss Shufflebottom smiled at me.

"I know, Sabrina. I know."

Once she'd left, I turned to the buffoon beside me. "I'm going to draw my picture now at that table, so you'll know where I'll be."

I was still terrified, but I didn't want Bonzo to know that. Uncle Ernie always said I should never allow myself to feel bullied by bullies. That's what they want. Bullies should never get what they want.

I sat next to Charlie, who was drawing his face with far too much hair.

"Why are you drawing a shaggy dog?"

"Hey, that's me," he said.

"It's you with a shaggy dog sitting on your head."

I could tell that I had gone too far. Charlie was very

sensitive, which I didn't really understand because he was smart and talented in almost every subject.

He should be super-confident, instead of shy.

"You don't have to sit here and make fun of my drawing. You can go and sit with Liam. We both know he's cooler than me."

"I don't want to sit with cool boys, I want to sit with you."

"Oh thanks."

What was wrong with me? I was behaving like Bonzo and constantly saying the wrong things. I wasn't thinking properly. I was too distracted. I had tried to make Charlie feel better and ended up making him feel ten times worse.

"I'm sorry, Charlie. You know what I mean. Liam is ok, really. But you are my friend, probably my best ..."

I bet we were both glad the Future Earth exhibition was pitch-black. My cheeks were burning hot.

Bonzo was still buzzing around me, like a fly around doggy poop. I had to get him away from me. And I wanted to cheer up Charlie. Maybe there was a clever way to do both.

I grabbed one of Charlie's detective maths puzzle books off the table. He took them everywhere. I found one of the toughest puzzles near the back of the book.

"Ah, excuse me, Bonzo. Could you help us with this, please?"

"What are you doing, Sabrina? I don't need help with my puzzles."

I winked at Charlie and whispered, "YouTube star. Bonzo recognises me, keeps following me everywhere, get him away from me."

"Got it."

Charlie winked back at me. But he was so excited that he winked at me with both eyes. I thought he had gone blind. He rubbed his eyes and took the book from me.

"Yeah, Bonzo, this maths puzzle, can you help me?"

Bonzo leaned over the table and frowned.

"I don't really like maths."

"It's a detective maths puzzle. It's more about murders and stuff."

"Oh, I like murders, hur hur."

"Ok, Bonzo, listen carefully," Charlie said. "There's been a murder."

"Where?" Bonzo said, looking over his shoulder.

"In the book."

"Oh, right, hur hur."

"There's been a murder. And the murderer left a brown hair at the crime scene."

"Did he cut it off?"

Very quietly, I tiptoed away from my chair.

"No, it just fell out," Charlie said. "Hairs fall out all the time."

"So he's a bald murderer?"

I stepped away from the table.

"No, he's not a bald murderer, Bonzo. He just lost one brown hair from his head, that's all, one brown hair."

"So he's a baby murderer?"

"Why is he a baby?"

"He's only got one brown hair."

"No, Bonzo, one brown hair fell off."

"So, he's a baby with no more hair! Poor baby! Poor bald baby!"

I moved to another table without Bonzo even noticing. He was still trying to understand Charlie's detective puzzle. They hadn't even got to the actual maths part yet and Bonzo was already confused.

But I had lost my spy.

I was alone in the dark. My waxwork figure was on the other side of the museum. For the first time all day, I could relax, just a little bit.

So I spent quite a lot of time on my self-portrait. I wanted to make my drawing as detailed as possible. My long, brown hair was just right. I made sure the eyes were brown. I worked hard on my small ears, my pointed chin and button nose. I don't like to brag. Royals do not brag. But it was probably the best drawing I had ever done.

Back at the Palace, I used to have art lessons with Miss Quick-Pants. And when I was really little, and it was too wet to go outside, me and Mummy and Daddy would scribble in colouring books at the kitchen table. Those were the best times.

I was having the worst time in the museum, but the drawing made me forget that, just for a few minutes. I was so proud of my masterpiece that I wanted to show Charlie, but he was still distracting Bonzo with his confusing murder talk.

So I pushed my drawing into the scanning machine and waited for my work to come alive.

Suddenly, my head was the size of a house. The screen blew up my picture until my face was bigger than my real body. My face was also 3D and walking through the fake city.

I was well chuffed with my artwork. The drawing was so realistic. It was like looking in a mirror.

And then I hated the artwork.

I hated it so badly I wanted to tear the giant screen down from the wall.

My head could've been stuck on top of anyone. A singer. An acrobat. A dentist. A lawyer. A zookeeper. Anything.

But I was wearing a frilly dress.

The dumb exhibition had shoved my head on a sparkly princess' dress.

CHAPTER ELEVEN

Everyone knows that you can't dress up like a princess, not at our age. That's a rule. We can still watch princess movies, but only the older ones about teenagers finding handsome princes in New York or Paris. We can't wear big pink dresses and those plastic tiaras with fake diamonds. We're not five years old.

So this was a serious crisis. If anyone saw me on the huge screen in that ridiculous dress, they'd take photos of me and stick them on Instagram. We're not supposed to have phones in class, but everyone hides them in their school bags, except Awful Agatha. She's never had a phone, not even one of her parents' old phones.

One of the drippy girls in our class once asked Awful Agatha why she didn't have a phone. Awful Agatha kicked her in the shins.

The girl didn't ask again.

I'm not allowed to be on Instagram anymore. No videos. No photos. Nothing. And it's so hard for anyone my age not to be on social media. Uncle Ernie said that my generation was born on social media and he's right. The other kids live on social media, but I can't because of the civil war in Mulakating.

But the Cabbage Patch bothered me the most. He was already suspicious. He must walk past my waxwork figure a hundred times every day. Even Bonzo was going to work it out eventually and he was really thick.

Luckily, Charlie was being his brilliant self. He was still explaining one of his detective maths puzzles to Bonzo. Charlie was talking. Bonzo was dribbling.

He really needed a tissue.

On the screen, my giant 3D head on top of a glittery, pink dress was wandering around the 3D city. I was just turning my back on the screen when I noticed another gigantic 3D figure walking towards the 3D version of me.

It was a marching soldier.

It was Liam the marching soldier.

I wished that I could disappear. But of course I couldn't, not with Awful Agatha around.

"Oh, look, Liam's gonna walk straight into Sabzy. She'll flip him over again."

Awful Agatha despised Liam. All right, she despised almost everyone, but she really loathed Liam for different reasons. She was upside down when it came to boys. The other, giggly girls had crushes on Liam because he was good-looking and played for the school football team and his father had a job that made quite a bit of money. But Awful Agatha hated him because he was handsome, talented and rich.

Charlie didn't get it, but I understood. Awful Agatha didn't like Liam for having all the things that she didn't have, things that other students in our school thought were really important.

They weren't, not to me anyway, but Awful Agatha wasn't interested in what I believed. She was interested in annoying Liam. She was pointing at his marching soldier and my princess on the massive screen and shouting.

"Let's see if Liam gets beaten up again. We can watch it on the big TV. Go on, Sabs. Flip him over again."

Some of the students laughed, even though Awful Agatha wasn't being really funny. But they laughed because they were the lucky ones. She was not picking on them. She was picking on Liam.

"Go on, Sabzy, smash his face in," said Awful Agatha, waving her fist at the screen.

Finally, Miss Shufflebottom decided to do something. She got really cross. Well, she got really cross for Miss Shufflebottom. She raised her voice a tiny bit.

"Er, please stop using such threatening language. There will be no smashing of faces in here."

"Not in here, Miss. On screen. Look. Liam and Sabrina. He loves her. But she hates him. She'll flip him over if he gets too close."

"Shut your fat gob, Agatha."

Liam was on his feet and sprinting towards Awful Agatha. He was obviously furious because he wasn't thinking properly.

Boys can't hit girls, not in schools. Well, boys can't hit girls anywhere, but especially in schools. That's another rule. Even if the boy wins the fight, he loses the fight, like, forever. No one wants to be known around the school as the boy who picks fights with girls. And smart boys don't pick fights with Awful Agatha.

It's like diving into the ocean and picking a fight with a shark.

Most girls aren't like Awful Agatha. Most girls, when they see an angry boy running towards them, panic and get out of the way.

But Awful Agatha stood her ground. "Yeah, you wanna go? You wanna go, Liam? Come on then, weasel face."

She raised her fists. Liam slowed down. He must have got his brain back. I think he'd just realised that he was going to get humiliated twice in one day by two different girls.

But Mr Cumberlatch came to Liam's rescue. He stepped between them and stretched his arms out. He looked like the letter T.

"There will be no fighting in my museum," he said.

"Yes, sir."

Liam sounded so relieved. Awful Agatha didn't.

"But I was gonna punch him right in the nose."

The Cabbage Patch's bulging veins in his neck looked ready to splatter blood all over Awful Agatha.

"Listen, young lady, they'll be no punching in my Future Earth exhibition."

"What about one kick between his legs?"

"No."

"You're lucky," Awful Agatha whispered at Liam.

"Shut up."

"You shut up. Everybody knows you've got a crush on

Sabrina and she beat you up in the Planetarium."

"No, she didn't. And why would I have a crush on her? She looks like a baby in that dress."

Liam pointed at the gigantic, interactive screen behind them. He carried on arguing with Awful Agatha until Miss Shufflebotton and Miss Cannington sent them both back to their seats and told them to draw something else.

But the Cabbage Patch never moved.

He was stuck still like a statue.

He never even blinked.

He was watching me, not me sitting at a table and keeping my head down, but me on the screen in a pink princess' dress. He gazed at my fantastic self-portrait on top of a random princess' body.

"No, it can't be," he whispered to himself. "It can't be."

He flicked his head around, like a snake attacking a baby lizard on one of those nature documentaries.

"Where are you?"

His eyes zigzagged all over the place until he found me in a corner.

"Yes, there you are," he said.

The Cabbage Patch had a horrible grin on his face.

"I know who you are now. And I'm very pleased to meet you at last."

He pushed a couple of kids out of the way and headed for the exit.

"Bonzo, take the class to the Chamber of Nightmares. I'm going to the Royalty Exhibition to check on a certain princess."

CHAPTER TWELVE

The Future Earth exhibition was a blur. I was moving so quickly. I had to catch Mr Cumberlatch. I didn't have a clue what I was doing, but I'd think of something along the way. Bravery was the best way forward. That was another of Uncle Ernie's sayings. I wasn't even sure what he meant. He didn't make much sense at the best of times. But I figured that if I was brave now, the idea might come later. All I knew was I needed another lie, another excuse for flying out of another exhibition.

Charles looked up from his detective maths puzzle as I whizzed past.

"Where are you going, Sabrina?"

"YouTube star emergency," I said, and kept on running.

Bonzo saw me chasing his boss. So he started chasing after me!

He wasn't supposed to be chasing me. He was supposed to be in charge. The Cabbage Patch had told Bonzo to take the class to the Chamber of Nightmares, but Bonzo wasn't very bright.

So the Cabbage Patch was chasing after a waxwork figure of me, I was chasing after the Cabbage Patch and Bonzo was chasing after the real me.

It was totally insane.

Bonzo's breathing was so loud. I thought a dragon was behind me.

"You've got to stay here, hur, hur," Bonzo said.

He tried to grab my shoulder, but just missed. He was getting closer though. I saw the Cabbage Patch disappear through the exit. He was gone. He was going to catch me, the other me, the waxwork me in the Royalty Exhibition. I felt Bonzo's fingers brush against my blazer. His breathing was right in my ear. He was going to stop me. I needed a miracle. I needed something. Anything.

So Liam burped, really loudly, right in Bonzo's face.

Well, I didn't need that.

At least, I thought I didn't need that.

Liam just appeared from nowhere and stood in front of Bonzo and burped. It was probably the longest and loudest burp I had ever heard. Liam's burps could go on forever. At the school canteen one day, he drank a full glass of lemonade and burped for 27 seconds. He told everyone that 27 seconds was a world record for a boy of his age. No one believed him, but it was the longest burp that I'd ever heard.

But his burp inside the Future Earth exhibition was even longer. His burp made Bonzo stop. I had a quick look over my shoulder.

"That's a great burp, hur hur," Bonzo said.

"Thanks, we were having a burping competition."

Liam pointed to the boys standing around him.

"Do you want to try?"

Bonzo hopped up and down like a rabbit. He was so excited.

"Yeah. I love burping, hur hur."

As Bonzo and the other boys burped, Liam glanced over at me.

"Go," he whispered.

I nodded and realised I was doing something really crazy for me. I was smiling at Liam, but not in the way I smile at Charlie, Uncle Ernie or Awful Agatha. This was a different smile, one that I'd never used before, not even for my parents.

I might have been smiling at him in *that* way.

My belly was all tight and squelchy. I blamed Uncle Ernie's cooking. He had made a lousy cheese pizza the night before. Yeah, that's what it was. I couldn't be thinking about what had really caused my knotted stomach.

But I was free. I was out of the Future Earth exhibition and into the long corridor.

But the corridor was packed. Millions of people swarmed around me like flies. There were old people. Young people. Families. School parties. Foreign tourists. I had never squeezed my way through such a big crowd before.

At the Palace, Uncle Ernie used his earpiece to tell the other handymen with earpieces to move people aside whenever there was a royal visit. I thought about using my aikido or my taekwondo, but I knew that wasn't a very royal thing to do. And it would take too long. Fencing would've been much quicker, but strangers should never be slashed with sabres in public.

And then I spotted the Cabbage Patch! He was heading into the Royalty Exhibition!

"Mr Cumberlatch, please, wait," I shouted.

But there was no chance of him hearing me over the noise of visitors yakking on about their favourite royal dresses and the prettiest queens. The museum staff were no better. I had to push past so many cleaners. They were mopping the floors, washing the walls, polishing the door handles and making a real mess. One of them almost hit me with his really long trolley. It was chaos.

At the Royalty Exhibition, there was a sign at the entrance:

The museum is sorry for any disruption at the Royalty Exhibition. A pest control expert issued a false alarm. The museum is pleased to announce that the exhibition is now open. There have been no sightings of any pests of any kind. And the museum entomologists would like to stress that there really is no such insect as the Norwegian Death Clock Beetle.

Uncle Ernie was like a big, grey-haired bomb. He caused a huge explosion wherever he went. But I couldn't think about him now. I had to focus and think of a plan. The Cabbage Patch was just ahead of me. What could I say? How could I wiggle my way out of this one? I ran different ideas through my head as I ran towards him. My heart was thumping, but I kept going, through the arched entrance.

Behind glass cases, there were crowns and gowns and dresses and jewels from different royal families. I didn't want to look because I was scared of losing Mr Cumberlatch.

But I really didn't want to look for a more depressing reason.

My life was in this room, my real life. There were dresses like mine. There were tiaras like mine. There were parents like mine.

And there were my parents.

I saw them.

They were inside a golden frame, just as they were on the walls of the Palace. But they were black and white in this photograph, smiling on their wedding day. They looked so happy together.

So I stopped.

I gave up.

I didn't care anymore.

I didn't want to lie anymore. I just wanted to see them, even if it was inside a wrinkled old photo. I didn't even care if I was arrested and sent back to Mulakating. At least I could see my parents, one more time, like all normal children should.

No child on this planet should be separated from Mum and Dad. People always think it's easier for richer families when children are taken away from their parents, but it's not. Money doesn't matter, does it? Rich or poor, it's still rubbish. Children want to grow up with Mum and Dad. They want to see them as often as possible and do normal things like go to the movies and eat popcorn or play in the park or make each other laugh at dinner time. Parents and children are like salt and pepper or macaroni and cheese or knives and forks.

They should go together. Always.

I stood in front of the photograph for ages. I wasn't bothered if all the clocks stopped. I was ready to stay there all day, staring at Mummy and Daddy, stuck in that golden frame, like they were trapped together in prison.

But I was tapped on the shoulder.

"I know why you're here."

I looked up at two dark, hairy caves. They were the Cabbage Patch's long nostrils.

"Come with me."

He tugged my blazer at the elbow and guided me across the Royalty Exhibition, away from my parents, away from my daydreaming.

I used to think that it was impossible to hate anyone as much as I used to hate Awful Agatha. But the Cabbage Patch had changed my mind. He had taken me away from my parents. He had taken me away from my daydreaming.

He had taken me away from my other life, my better life.

He had switched on this light in my brain, and I now only saw red.

"Don't touch me. You're not my teacher," I said through gritted teeth.

He obviously realised how furious I was because he let me go.

"Just follow me please."

I did as I was told, but not because I was worried about Mr Cumberlatch. One aikido jab in the ribs would take care of him, but I knew I couldn't make a scene in the museum, especially not in the Royalty Exhibition. Security guards and tour guides would be around us like ants on a sticky bun.

"I am taking you to your own exhibit, young lady. I saw you coming in and I thought, why not give her a personal tour of her own display, the Princess Power display. We're very proud of it. We've got ten young princesses from around the world, waxwork figures, to show how monarchies are becoming younger and more modern."

The grand hall of the Royalty Exhibition was enormous, but I could see them in the distance. The princesses were lined up like statues at the back of the grand hall, all wearing their native costumes.

The Cabbage Patch skipped along the polished floorboards.

"Yes, I couldn't figure it out at first. Then I saw you in that princess dress and, by the way, you are a very talented artist. But when I saw you on that wall in 3D, everything became clear."

We stopped in front of the Princess Power display. I think my heart stopped, too. My eyes were really stinging, but I wasn't going to weep, not for him.

"Look, I don't understand. My name is Sabrina Parslowe. I come from a small family and I live in a small town ..."

"Yes, yes, yes," he interrupted. "And you live in a small house inside a small shoe. Please. That's not who you are. This is who you really are!"

The Cabbage Patch raised his hands towards nothing.

"Who am I?"

He was pointing at an empty space on the platform.

"Where are you?"

"I'm right here."

"No, where are you up there?"

He climbed onto the Princess Power platform and dashed along the stage counting the waxwork princesses.

"Six, seven, eight, nine ... nine? There should be ten, not nine. There should be ten princesses. I've lost a princess. I've lost you!"

"I'm down here."

"No, I've lost you up here."

"I never went up there."

"Don't treat me like a fool. You have stolen the waxwork figure of yourself!"

"But I was with you the whole time."

And that was the truth. I really was with Mr Cumberlatch the whole time.

But the museum cleaner with the long trolley wasn't.

CHAPTER THIRTEEN

I was definitely going to have a heart attack. I ran through the Royalty Exhibition like a lunatic. I didn't even stop for another peek at Mummy and Daddy's photograph. This was no time for sentimentality. I had to be like those rigid waxworks and show a bit of a princess power. I left Mr Cumberlatch moaning about a thief in his museum.

He was terrified. I wasn't surprised. I don't know much about managing a museum, but I'm pretty sure it's a big deal when a life-sized waxwork figure goes missing in broad daylight.

No one normal steals a life-sized waxwork figure in broad daylight.

But Uncle Ernie wasn't normal.

Just the other day, he wrestled with a stranger on our doorstep. He tied the stranger's hands and demanded to know the name of his spy network.

The stranger was delivering my cheese pizza.

Uncle Ernie let him off with a warning and told him to bring extra garlic bread next time.

I didn't get the chance to recognise the museum cleaner with the long trolley, but it made perfect sense now.

Uncle Ernie loved disguises. I think he just loves dressing up, but his disguises always seem to work. To me, he's obviously

Uncle Ernie in a bad wig or a dodgy dress. Whenever I make fun of his disguises, he taps the side of his nose and says the same thing: *They see only what we want them to see.*

I was beginning to understand what he meant now. The museum visitors didn't see an imposter pinching a statue. They saw a cleaner in a museum uniform taking away an exhibit for cleaning. Why would they stop him?

But Uncle Ernie was like a cat in a litter tray. He always left a mess behind.

When I tried to leave the Royalty Exhibition, the big archway entrance was blocked with scared visitors saying crazy things.

"I'm not going in there," an old lady said. "That place is full of *Norwegian Death Clock Beetles.*"

"I can assure you, madam, there is no such thing as a Norwegian Death Clock Beetle," a stressed tour guide insisted.

"Then why did you fumigate the place for a beetle that doesn't exist," said the old lady's even older husband.

"We're not sure who that pest control officer was."

"Wait? So it was a secret mission?" another woman shouted.

"No, madam, we just didn't know about it."

"And you didn't know about the Norwegian Death Choc Beetles," said the old lady.

"They were called Norwegian Death *Clock* Beetles, madam."

"So they are real! We're gonna get eaten alive by killer beetles!"

The place went nuts. There were dumbstruck tourists running in every direction. There were screaming tour guides chasing after screaming old people. And there were young children screaming because, let's face it, they're always screaming.

But luckily, the screaming was a perfect distraction. As the visitors ran around, a gap opened up at the archway entrance and I squeezed myself through. In the distance, I saw Uncle Ernie in his cleaner's uniform, shoving the long trolley into a broom cupboard.

I sprinted the last bit and ducked into the broom cupboard before anyone had a chance to see me.

Now I screamed.

The room was pitch-black and I walked straight into a cupboard shelf.

"Argh," I cried.

"Sabrina?"

"Uncle Ernie?"

"No, I'm the Ghost of Museum Broom Cupboards."

"Really?"

"No, of course not. I'm Uncle Ernie."

"Well, I don't know, do I? I can't see a thing."

"Oh, right."

Uncle Ernie switched on his cleaner's torch. His face glowed. He was smiling. He loved every second of a crisis.

"But my sarcasm is getting good, right?"

"Not really."

"Thanks. Anyway, what are we going to do about you?"

"I'll have to run back to the class. They are going to the Chamber of Nightmares."

"No, not you, I meant the other you."

He pointed his torch over my shoulder. I turned round. "Argh!"

I was standing in front of myself. It was the freakiest thing ever.

"There's your real ghost of the museum broom cupboard."

"That's not funny, Uncle Ernie."

"It is a little bit funny."

"No, it's not. And what are we supposed to do now then? Stay in here all day with my stolen waxwork figure?"

"Easy. I've got it all worked out. You can go back to your class. Complete your tour and I'll stay in here with the other you, the waxy one. When you're safely on the school bus, I'll put the waxy you back with the other princesses."

"You can't do that!"

"Of course I can. I can get wifi on my phone in here. I can watch YouTube."

"No, I mean, what if someone comes in?"

"They can't."

Uncle Ernie held up a long silver key in front of the torchlight. He seemed so proud of it.

"Made this myself. Universal key. It can open almost any lock in the world. How do you think I got into the museum storeroom and borrowed this uniform?"

I shoved my fingers in my ears.

"Lalalalalalalah ... I don't want to hear this! You are a thief!"

Uncle Ernie grinned at me.

"Ah, but I'm not stealing anything. I'm just borrowing this

stuff, just like when you borrow a book from the library. Going to the library isn't a crime, is it?"

"It is if you take their pest control gun and spray the library with insecticide!"

"You really are good at that sarcasm, aren't you?"

"Uncle Ernie!"

"Look, we didn't create this situation, did we? We're just dealing with each problem, one at a time, day by day, all right?"

"Yeah, all right."

"Good. Do you want to hug?"

"Ew, no, you still stink of fogging spray."

"Thanks. Right, you better get back to your group before you're missed."

I almost left.

I was so close.

I was standing at the door. I had even grabbed the handle, when an announcement blared out across the entire museum.

"Ladies and gentlemen, do not be alarmed, but we are temporarily closing all entrances and exits to the museum."

It was the Cabbage Patch. His voice boomed through every speaker on every floor and he wasn't done yet.

"Visitors are required to stay where they are for the time being as we conduct a thorough security check. One of our exhibits appears to have been stolen."

Uncle Ernie and I were trapped in a dark, filthy broom cupboard, with the stolen exhibit that everyone in the museum was now looking for.

CHAPTER FOURTEEN

Once I was ready, Uncle Ernie pushed me out of the broom cupboard.

"You know what to do," he said. "Remember, they see only what we want them to see, and you look perfect. So be brave and get it done."

He slammed the door behind me.

But I didn't know what to do. Well, all right, I did, but the idea was ludicrous, even by Uncle Ernie's standards.

For the plan to work, I needed a distraction, a crazy, over-the-top distraction to get the Cabbage Patch out of the way.

I was halfway down the corridor when I heard what should have been a crazy, over-the-top distraction. But it was even crazier than that.

"Good morning, ladies and gentlemen. This is a message for museum guide, Mr Cumberlatch. Could he please make his way to the Chamber of Nightmares, where Bonzo has poked himself in the eye with a pencil."

Uncle Ernie's voice echoed around the museum. I don't know how he managed to hack into the speaker system. And I don't know why he was using such a posh voice either. But he loved playing different characters. In fact, he loved getting into character so much that he often forgot to snap out of character.

"And while I have your attention, ladies and gentlemen, let me take the opportunity to tell you about our current two-for-one special offer in the gift shop with our staff. If you buy one staff member, you'll get the other one free! Ha ha, just a little museum humour there."

The thing was, Uncle Ernie did make people laugh. I kept jogging past tourists giggling at his nonsensical commentary. He was a useful distraction, I suppose. No one took any notice of me as I made my way back to the Royalty Exhibition.

Considering I never wanted to go anywhere near the Royalty Exhibition, I couldn't seem to stay away.

I was already fed up with the place.

But I kept going. And so did Uncle Ernie on the museum's speaker system.

"And don't forget to visit our Tombs of Ancient Egypt, where some of the exhibits are four thousand years old, almost as old as our toilets."

He made me cringe. But his plan was sort of working. He had tricked the Cabbage Patch to get him out of my way and distracted everyone else with his bad jokes.

By the time I reached the Royalty Exhibition, I needed a drink and a cheese sandwich. But I didn't have either. I had left my rucksack with Awful Agatha, which meant I probably had an empty water bottle and no cheese sandwiches left.

I missed Awful Agatha a little bit, which was weird, right?

I had spent so much time running around the museum like a headless chicken that I had left my friends behind. I couldn't wait to join them at the Chamber of Nightmares.

Nothing inside that chamber could be as scary as my real-life nightmare outside.

But I didn't think I'd make it to the Chamber of Nightmares.

I didn't have enough time. I was too late.

Mr Cumberlatch had already returned to the Royalty Exhibition. He was at the other end of the grand hall, near the archway entrance, but he was closing in fast.

I wasn't ready.

I hadn't reached my hiding place yet.

I lifted the uncomfortable dress and ran faster until I found the right spot.

The exact spot.

Luckily, there was no one around so I could hide in peace.

But the Cabbage Patch's long, lanky legs whizzed across the polished floor. He galloped like a clumsy giraffe. He was going to see me.

He was definitely going to see me.

The plan wasn't going to work. It was going to be a big fat failure and I was about to be discovered.

I took a deep breath and froze, but my heart was hammering away at my ribcage like a massive bell.

The Cabbage Patch headed my way and took out his walkie-talkie.

"No, Bonzo hasn't shoved a pencil up his nose," he said into the walkie-talkie. "No, I don't know who's coming up with all these pranks. It's probably Bonzo! You remember that time we caught him eating a museum brochure? We told him the brochure was 'full of good stuff' so he started eating it."

I heard his footsteps. He was so close.

He was standing in front of me.

"Yes, I'm back in the Royalty Exhibition now. I'm telling you, the waxwork figure has been stolen ... wait, it's back. The waxwork figure is back! No, I'm not going mad. It's right in front of me, on the Princess Power stage. No, I don't need a lie down. Yes, I'll get back to my school group. I'm telling you, the waxwork figure wasn't there before and now it's back. Something very fishy is going on here."

When he turned away, I finally blinked.

I was really proud of myself. I stood and stared for ages and I never moved, even when that ugly pink dress made my back all itchy.

And I never closed my eyes once.

Waxworks are not supposed to blink.

CHAPTER FIFTEEN

The next part of the plan was easy. Well, it was easy compared to the last part of the plan. I jumped off the stage when no one was looking, pulled off the pink dress and handed it to a museum window cleaner behind the Princess Power display. He hid the dress in his empty bucket.

Of course, the window cleaner was Uncle Ernie. He had to get the dress back onto the waxwork figure in the broom cupboard and I had to get to the Chamber of Nightmares.

But I had to beat Mr Cumberlatch. I had watched enough superhero movies to know that the trick to protecting a secret identity was to pretend to be in two different places at the same time.

If Princess Sabrina Valence in the pink dress had been in the Royalty Exhibition when Sabrina Parslowe in her school uniform was in the Chamber of Nightmares, then the Cabbage Patch would be fooled.

Uncle Ernie handed over my school blazer and tie. My shirt and skirt were a bit screwed up after being squashed beneath the princess dress, but no one would notice.

My real issue was *me*, the other me. There were two Sabrinas in the building. Actually, there were three at that particular moment.

There was the me that was trying to get to the Chamber

of Nightmares before the Cabbage Patch. There was the me that had just stood still and pretended to be a waxwork figure. And then there was the waxwork me stuffed in a broom cupboard and missing her pink dress.

I had to keep all three of me separated.

The confusing thing was that the waxwork of me was actually my real life—and the real, human version of me was living a fake life. But I couldn't worry about that now. I just had to outrun the Cabbage Patch.

Luckily, I had a super sneaky Uncle Ernie.

As I took off, he pulled out his walkie-talkie from his cleaner's overalls.

"This is an urgent message for Mr Cumberlatch," he said. "Please report to the Future Earth exhibition. Bonzo has eaten one of the crayons."

The visitors all around me were laughing. Even I chuckled, which wasn't helpful as I was already struggling to breathe.

But I made it, just about, thanks to Uncle Ernie.

I beat the Cabbage Patch back to the Chamber of Nightmares.

The exhibit was dark and full of cobbled streets. The place really was spooky. A sign said that the town was based on the East End of London in Victorian times, when crime and murder could be found in every alleyway. The streets were foggy and filled with smoke. Waxwork figures in long back coats and top hats peered through cracked windows. Their eyes were blood red. Their teeth were crooked and pointy. Cackling laughter filled the gloomy streets. Screaming and fleeing footsteps could be heard in the alleyways.

There was another sign written in scribbly red ink:

Be warned. The Chamber of Nightmares is not for the weak, the scared or the timid. Children enter the chamber at their own risk. This is a place of fear and terror.

"I love this place," said Awful Agatha.

I heard her voice through a crowd of shivering people. The Chamber of Nightmares was freezing. I squeezed through and found the rest of the class.

Miss Cannington was at the front of the group, walking alongside Bonzo. Miss Shufflebottom was at the back, keeping an eye on Awful Agatha.

On tiptoes, I crept up on them, hoping they wouldn't notice.

"Where have you been?"

Awful Agatha was so loud.

"Yes, where have you been, Sabrina?"

"Toilet."

"For so long?"

"It was the other kind of toilet, Miss Shufflebottom."

"She went for a poo, Miss. A poo."

"Yes, all right, Agatha. I get it. Are you all right now, Sabrina?"

"I'm fine, Miss Shufflebottom."

That was unusual for me. I'd actually spoken the truth. All right, I wasn't completely fine. But Uncle Ernie was working on the waxwork situation and I was back in my school uniform and standing in the dark.

Plus, I got to listen to the silliest museum guide in the world.

Bonzo stopped in front of an old barbershop.

"This is, er, an old barbershop, hur, hur," he said. "The barber used to kill people in here."

Some of the children gasped, but Charlie put his hand up, looking like he was ready to burst from the excitement.

"Sweeney Todd," he said.

"Who is?"

"No, Sweeney Todd was a fictional character. He was a barber in London who killed people and then baked the bodies in meat pies."

"Ooh, I'll have a meat pie," said Awful Agatha.

Bonzo pointed at the barbershop.

"Yeah, well, he's over here. Another dead bloke is over there. And in this corner is, er ... another dead bloke. And over there is ... let me see."

"Another dead bloke?" said Liam.

"Yeah, how did you know? Have you been here before?"

The class started sniggering. Bonzo ignored them.

"This place is full of dead people, hur hur. There's another dead one up here."

Bonzo picked his nose.

"There's a dead person up your nose," said Liam.

Liam's friends all laughed at his lame joke.

"Ha ha, very funny. Now look here, on your left are loads of famous murderers and on your right are even more famous murderers. So pick your favourite murderer and, er, draw a picture of his scary face."

Miss Cannington stood in front of Bonzo.

"Wait, Mr Bonzo. I don't think that's appropriate."

"Oh yeah, you're right. I didn't bring any paper with me. Ok, everyone take selfies with their favourite murderers instead."

"I'll take it from here, Bonzo."

I was shivering. And it wasn't the air-conditioning. The Cabbage Patch was back. He shoved Bonzo out of the way. Bonzo stood beside the barbershop and picked his nose. The Cabbage Patch stood in front of the class and glared at me.

"Sorry for the interruptions. I can promise you there won't be any more of them for the rest of this tour."

He stepped into the crowd. The children stood aside, creating a path on the cobbled street.

"And have you all been enjoying the tour in my absence?"

The others cheered and said the right things. But the Cabbage Patch ignored their excitement. He kept walking towards me.

"And you, young lady? Have you enjoyed the Chamber of Nightmares?"

"Yes, sir."

"Mr Cumberlatch."

"Yes, Mr Cumberlatch."

He towered over my head like a crooked Eiffel Tower. My neck ached just peering up at him.

"And what specifically have you enjoyed about this exhibition?"

I couldn't think. My mind had gone blank. Obviously, I couldn't tell the truth, that I'd only been there 30 seconds longer than he had.

I tried to use my peripheral vision, looking through the sides of my face like the ponies did back at the Palace stables. But I couldn't read any signs.

"There's no need to look for what we're about to see. Tell me what you've already seen in the Chamber of Nightmares because you've been here the whole time, right?"

He leaned over. His nostril hairs flickered in my face.

And then, from the corner of my eye, I spotted a maths detective puzzle book waving in the air. Charlie mouthed the words "Sweeney Todd" at me.

"Sweeney Todd," I blurted out.

"I beg your pardon?"

"Sweeney Todd. I like Sweeney Todd, he was a fictional character, that one over there, the waxwork figure in the barbershop. He was a barber in London who killed people and then baked the bodies in meat pies."

"I'd love a meat pie," said Awful Agatha.

The Cabbage Patch ignored her and focused on me.

"You haven't blinked once," he whispered. "Policemen say that liars don't blink because they are concentrating so much on getting their story straight. Maybe you are lying. Or maybe, you're just very, very good at not blinking. In fact, you could almost be a waxwork figure, couldn't you?"

CHAPTER SIXTEEN

Bonzo wouldn't leave me alone. It was so obvious that the Cabbage Patch had sent his orangutan spy to follow me everywhere. But I didn't care. As long as we stayed away from the Royalty Exhibition, that was fine by me. Plus, it was funny watching Awful Agatha and Charlie argue in the Chamber of Nightmares.

Charlie thought the detectives who caught the famous murderers were amazing.

Awful Agatha thought the murderers were amazing.

And Liam still seemed to think I was amazing.

He followed me around as much as Bonzo. Both of them kept pestering me.

"Can I hold your hand in the Chamber of Nightmares?" Liam asked.

"I'm going to stay with you in the Chamber of Nightmares," Bonzo said.

"I love the Chamber of Nightmares," Awful Agatha said.

She was really excited. She also looked a bit pale, like ghosts inside the Chamber of Nightmares. They weren't really ghosts, just waxwork figures with white bed sheets thrown over their heads, but they terrified poor Charlie.

"Are you ok, Agatha?" I whispered.

"Shut up, Sabby, I wanna hear this bit."

"That doesn't make any sense. You never want to listen to anything educational."

"Yeah, but that one there chopped off the head of that one over there."

That made perfect sense.

"But you still look very pale."

"Yeah, well, you look like an orange."

"Why are you calling me an orange?"

"You called me a pear."

"Not pear. Pale. Your face is very pale, almost see though, like water."

"Are you making fun of me?"

Awful Agatha always stood up straight when she felt threatened. She was like one of those meerkats—fighting was her answer for everything. It made the other girls scared of her. It made me feel sorry for her.

"Of course I'm not making fun of you."

"You're saying I look like pears and water, or pears in water, or something like that. Are you saying I've got a face like pear juice?"

"No, I don't even know what pear juice looks like. I just think, you know, you look, kind of hungry."

"Well, I'm not hungry. I had your cheese sandwich before. So shut up."

"Do you want another one?"

"Yeah, all right."

We ran off giggling. I wanted to get away from Bonzo's spying, even if it was just for a few minutes. Bonzo tried to come with us, but I told him that we were off to the girls' toilets and if he stepped into a girl's toilet while I was in there, he would get fired. And Awful Agatha told him that if he stepped into a girl's toilet while she was in there, she would chop his head off.

She wouldn't. She was just obsessed with the Chamber of Nightmares.

We tapped on the door of another broom cupboard next to the Chamber of Nightmares. No one answered so we tiptoed inside. The tiny room was pitch-black. There were lots of shelves full of paint tins and old sheets. I thought about switching on the light of my phone, but remembered that we weren't supposed to bring phones to school.

That wasn't the real reason though. Awful Agatha was the only girl in our class who didn't have a phone. She usually went ballistic when the other girls showed off their phones in school.

"It's dark in here," I said.

"I like the dark. Give us a sandwich, Sabzy."

We sat on the floor next to some mops and buckets. I fumbled through my rucksack until I found something soft and squidgy. I handed over a sweaty cheese sandwich. Our hands touched and she pulled away really quickly.

No one touched Awful Agatha at school. It was one of her many rules.

She swallowed huge chunks in one go. The sandwich disappeared so fast, she didn't even seem to chew.

"Wow, you must be hungry."

"No, I wanna get back to the Chamber of Nightmares."

That was a lie. She was just starving.

I think she probably knew that I knew she was lying. But we both pretended that she was telling the truth. This happens quite a lot with us. We both have these annoying family secrets that we refuse to talk about.

"Did you have any dinner last night?"

"Of course, I had dinner last night. What sort of stupid question is that?"

She nudged me in the shoulder. I had broken one of her rules: No talk about family or home.

"Yeah, of course you did."

"Yeah, of course I did. Idiot. Got another cheese sandwich?"

I gave her my last cheese sandwich.

"You got any more for yourself?"

"Yeah, loads."

I was so good at lying now, even Awful Agatha couldn't tell the difference. I tried to change the subject.

"This museum is boring," I said.

Awful Agatha sat up straight. I knew I had said the right thing. She thought everything was boring.

"Yeah, the Planetarium was rubbish, didn't understand a word of that show about space, the other one was for soppy kids who like scribbling stupid pictures and I don't even want to go into the princess thing. We're not little kids."

"Yeah, I don't want to see the princesses either. They're so lame."

"The Chamber of Nightmares is all right though."

"Yeah, a bit scary though."

"Not for me. I'm used to it."

Awful Agatha stopped chewing for a second. She looked worried, like she was thinking about something else.

"Have you been here before?" I asked.

"It feels like I live here."

"What?"

"Nothing. Come on. I want to get back to the murderers."

She stood up quickly. Too quickly.

She turned and bashed her forehead against one of the metal shelves.

"Ow," she shouted.

Actually, she shouted more than just "ow". She shouted lots of rude words that a princess simply cannot write in a journal.

She rubbed her eyebrow.

"I think my head is bleeding. It is definitely bleeding, stupid shelf."

She kicked the shelf.

"Ow, now I've hurt my foot, stupid, stupid shelf."

She didn't say "stupid" twice either, but I'm not writing what she really said.

I tried to have a look at her injuries, but she pushed me away.

"Don't touch me."

"I'm not touching you, but I can't see if you're bleeding in the dark, can I?"

"Well, find the light switch then."

I was getting desperate. Awful Agatha was shouting out all the foul words in her vocabulary. She had so many foul words in her vocabulary—if our school allowed her to write English essays in bad language, she'd be an A-grade student.

I had to do something. Busybodies would hear her cries and stick their noses into our private business. Without thinking, I took out my phone and switched on the light.

"Hey, you've got a phone."

"Yeah, well, stand still."

Awful Agatha did as she was told, mostly. She didn't stop swearing though.

"There's no blood. I think you might have a bump though, just above your eye."

"Stupid shelf."

Awful Agatha kicked the shelf again, which caused the tins of paint to jump in the air. Then she kicked the buckets, which made the mops clatter against each other.

And then, in a really childish tantrum, she grabbed a white sheet on a shelf behind me and threw it to the floor. Then she screamed.

I had never heard Awful Agatha scream before.

This was a girl who'd just watched waxwork figures pretend to kill each other in the Chamber of Nightmares and thought it was cool.

But she didn't sound terrified or scared now. She was sort of shocked and confused. At first I thought the bump on her forehead had turned her brain to jelly. She kept talking gibberish.

"It's you behind you. It's you behind you."

She pointed over my shoulder. Her eyes were wide and freaky.

"There are two of you. How can you be standing in front of you?"

I didn't need to turn round. I knew exactly what she was pointing at.

Uncle Ernie had dumped the other me in the worst place possible.

CHAPTER SEVENTEEN

Uncle Ernie always says I have an answer for everything. And if I don't, he gives me an answer for everything.

But he wasn't with me and I had no answer. Not for this. What could I say? Girls don't have waxwork figures of themselves inside fancy museums. Even if Uncle Ernie had been with me, what could he have said?

I was in a ridiculous situation with a suspicious girl who never believed anything anyone said anyway.

Awful Agatha kept pointing and repeating herself.

"You are behind you. You are behind you. Why are you behind you?"

"Stop shouting. They'll hear you outside. Are you still hungry?"

"I'm not stupid. We made a promise. No lying to each other."

"I'm not lying."

"You never told me you had a figure of yourself in the museum."

"You never asked me."

"Don't be sarcastic. You lied to me. They're always lying to me, at home. That's why I made you promise. No lies at school!"

Her face was turning a funny colour. She was that scary

mix of sad and furious, the worst kind of emotional mix for Awful Agatha. No one had any idea what she might do next when she was like this, not even her.

I took a deep breath, but it made no difference. My head had gone all gooey, like the cheap mac and cheese in the school canteen.

"You're right. Friends shouldn't lie to friends. I'll tell you the truth."

Part of me didn't want to do this. Uncle Ernie would be disappointed and I'd have to listen to his usual lecture about the safety and security of our royal family. But the other part of me couldn't be bothered anymore. I was sick of hiding in smelly broom cupboards like an escaped prisoner.

"Yeah, tell me the truth," said Awful Agatha.

"Ok, I will."

"Well, go on then."

"I am. Give me a chance ... ok, I'm not who you think I am."

"I think you're a moron."

"Seriously, Agatha, just listen. I'm not really Sabrina Parslowe. My real name is Sabrina. I mean, what I'm saying is, I'm—"

"SABRINA THE YOUTUBE STAR!"

The broom cupboard door flew open and a piercing light dazzled our eyes. We covered our faces and blinked. A toddler waddled into the broom cupboard.

I blinked again. It wasn't a toddler. It was Charlie! My hero!

I stepped forward to hug him, but he pulled a funny face and so did Awful Agatha and I remembered where I was. Girls don't hug boys at school. It's another one of those weird rules.

"Charlie, what are you doing here?"

He closed the door, stood on a bucket and took a long look at my waxwork figure's face.

"She does look like you. She's even wearing one of those frilly dresses. I've seen you in a dress like this in photos at your house."

I could see Awful Agatha losing her temper. She wanted to kick Charlie's bucket.

"Will someone please tell me what's going on?"

"I heard what you were saying outside so I came in to help."

"How could you hear us?"

"I was listening through the keyhole."

"Yeah, you're short enough," said Awful Agatha.

Charlie looked at the waxwork figure and then at me. He gave me a slightly embarrassed smile. It was kind of goofy and awkward.

"Wow, I didn't realise you were that famous, though. I didn't think they made statues of YouTube stars."

"It's not really a statue. It's just a cheap waxwork figure," I said.

Awful Agatha grabbed a paintbrush from the shelf.

"If someone doesn't tell me what's going on, I'm gonna stick this paintbrush up their nose."

She waved the paintbrush in front of Charlie's face. He made this yelping sound like a kitten. He started talking fast, far too fast for me to slow him down.

"Well, what happened was, one day, I went round Sabrina's house and I saw this photo of her dressed in a fancy costume and her dad, well, not her dad, her Uncle Ernie. She has an Uncle Ernie and he had all these computers for her. And she was really clever and, you know, the other thing, she's quite, you know, she looks good on camera. And she's always on computers and being mysterious and keeping secrets. But I'm brilliant at detective puzzles so I worked it out for myself. She's young, secretive and smart and goes to exotic places for photo shoots and she's always on the computer. So it's obvious, right? She's a YouTube star. But she's a private YouTuber. She has all her settings set to private. It's quite easy to do, you know. Are you going to stick that paintbrush up my nose?"

Awful Agatha dropped the paintbrush, which rattled loudly against a bucket. We were making too much noise.

She nodded at me, trying to be cool and laid-back, as if she wasn't impressed.

"So you're a YouTube star then?"

I shrugged my shoulders.

"That's all right, I suppose," said Awful Agatha. "What is a YouTube star?"

Charlie seemed genuinely surprised.

"Don't you watch YouTubers on your computer?"

"We don't have a computer."

Awful Agatha gritted her teeth. I knew where this was going.

"So what do you watch YouTube on? What do you use for the Internet?"

"We don't have the Internet at home."

"So how do you watch YouTube videos without the Internet?"

"I don't know, midget. How will you eat your dinner without your front teeth?"

Awful Agatha twisted her body. She was about to throw a punch at Charlie, and I could see it coming a mile away.

My aikido training took over. I stood between my friends and caught Awful Agatha's wrist, but made it look like I had bumped into her by accident.

"Ooh, sorry, Agatha. It's too dark in here."

"Clumsy idiot."

She knew I wasn't clumsy or an idiot.

"So you're famous then," she said, changing the subject.

"I'll tell you about it later. I promise. But we've got to get me out of here."

Charlie seemed confused.

"Which you? You, you or the other you?"

I tapped my chest.

"Me, me."

Now Awful Agatha looked confused.

"Who's Mimi? Isn't she that dopey-looking kid in Year One?"

"No, that's Minnie," said Charlie. "And I'm talking about the other Sabrina."

"There's only one Sabrina in our school."

"But there's two on this school trip!"

Charlie grabbed my waxwork figure under the chin.

"There's this one as well."

"And we can't be seen together," I said.

"Who can't be seen together? Me and you?" Awful Agatha said.

"No, me and me," I said, pointing at the waxwork figure. "This is waxwork me and I am the real me. Got it? This is fake me and this is me, me."

But I was wasting my time. I didn't need to say anything. They had already stopped. They were focused on the door of the broom cupboard. We all were.

Someone was turning the door handle.

"I know you're in there," said Bonzo, on the other side of the door.

We panicked, for a second, and then I had one of those flashes of inspiration.

"Quick, we can hide the other me. Grab that white sheet, Agatha."

The door was opening. Awful Agatha picked up the white sheet. Charlie leapt down from the bucket, standing away from the waxwork figure.

"Yeah, good idea, Sabrina," he said.

Charlie and I edged away from the waxwork figure.

Bonzo's silhouette slowly filled the doorway.

"Come out, come out, wherever you are, hur, hur," he said.

Awful Agatha held the sheet up.

"Ok, throw it," I whispered.

And she did. The white sheet floated through the air,

almost in slow motion. It really was a great shot—in the wrong direction!

She threw the sheet over the wrong me, the real me!

Bonzo had discovered Charlie and Awful Agatha hiding in a broom cupboard and standing next to a waxwork figure of their best friend.

CHAPTER EIGHTEEN

Sometimes, I'm a bit mean with Charlie. I know I am. He's not that annoying really and I'm not a nasty person. It's just that he can do daft things at daft times. The other day, I was really missing my parents, which was only natural, right? I couldn't tell Charlie why I was so moody so I stayed silent.

But Charlie can't stay silent. Ever. So he started going on about one of his maths detective puzzles, but he picked one that really turned my stomach, something about a father being kidnapped for ransom money. So I shouted at him.

When I shout at Charlie, he blushes and his bottom lip wobbles like a caterpillar. He feels bad. I feel bad. We both feel bad about each other.

But these arguments probably happen about 10 per cent of the time. The other 80 per cent is normal, everyday stuff, like hanging out in the school canteen and eating lunch together.

And then the other 10 per cent is the magical stuff.

That's when Charlie surprises me. That's when Charlie's overloaded brain comes to the rescue. And he really came to my rescue in the broom cupboard.

As Bonzo pushed the door open, Charlie dived on top of me!

Normally, he would've got a taekwondo kick somewhere painful, but he didn't dive on *me*. He dived on the other me.

He rugby-tackled the waxwork figure to the floor, clattering against the paint tins and mops and buckets.

"Oi, what are you doing in there?"

No one answered Bonzo. I was still hiding under my white sheet, standing perfectly still at the back of the broom cupboard. I had squeezed myself between two shelf-racks filled with junk. I couldn't see much through the sheet, just silhouettes and shadows mostly. It was dark, and Bonzo was squinting. Awful Agatha's teeth were easy to spot. She just stood there, grinning at Bonzo. Nothing made Awful Agatha happier than irritating someone in authority. I was sweating under the sheet behind the shelves. And Charlie was on the floor, half-hugging my waxwork figure.

Bonzo's hand ran up and down the wall like a spider, trying to find a light switch.

"Please don't," said Charlie.

"Please don't what?"

"No lights. She's sick again."

"Who?"

Bonzo took half a step into the broom cupboard. Charlie raised his hand.

"Be careful! She's just thrown up all over the floor."

Bonzo took half a step backwards.

"Who did?"

"Sabrina, the girl who fainted in the Planetarium, remember? She got too scared in the Chamber of Nightmares, so we brought her in here and she fainted."

For a split second, I thought about giving Charlie a huge

cuddle. But then I remembered that I was hiding under a dusty white sheet and cuddling boys was still a bit disgusting.

But his quick thinking was so smart. I had fainted before, so it made sense that I fainted a second time, right?

Maybe the Cabbage Patch wouldn't have fallen for Charlie's story, but Bonzo was about as bright as the broom cupboard.

"Oh no, I can't have any more sick kids on my tour," said Bonzo.

"She's not really sick. She just fainted."

"Yeah, she just fainted. That's all," said Awful Agatha, finally working out what Charlie was up to. She nodded enthusiastically—the girl loved any chance to tell a lie. "Yeah, she died."

Even through the white sheet, I could see Charlie fidgeting.

"No, she didn't die, Agatha," Charlie said, tapping the waxwork figure. "She just fainted. Remember? That's why she's so still."

"Oh, yeah. That's right. She's not dead. She's, you know, in a coma."

"What?" Bonzo shouted.

"Yeah, what?" Charlie said.

"She's in a coma, right, Charlie? She's not dead. She's just, like, nearly dead."

Bonzo grabbed his walkie-talkie off his belt.

"I'm gonna call an ambulance."

Charlie flapped his arms like a bird's wings.

"No, no, no. She's not nearly dead. She's just fainted. We will carry her to the water cooler. Come on Agatha, help me to lift her up."

Bonzo took another step into the dark broom cupboard.

"I will help you."

Charlie raised a hand to stop Bonzo.

"No, no. I must remind you of Section 10, Sub-section 6 of the 2008 Museum Guide, which says that sick students can only be handled by trained doctors and nurses, and not museum guides, unless they have a degree in medicine. Do you have a degree in medicine, Bonzo?"

"No, I don't have any medicine, except my hay fever tablets."

"Exactly. Please step aside, Bonzo."

Charlie and Awful Agatha were totally amazing. They even took another white sheet and wrapped it around the waxwork's body to hide the stiff, fake legs.

Charlie insisted that no one disturbed them on their way to the water cooler outside the toilets, just in case the waxwork me threw up in their faces. He also asked for no torches or unnecessary lights, as the other me had felt dizzy before fainting. The little genius had thought of everything.

Well, almost everything.

Charlie and Awful Agatha made it to the door and past Bonzo, with the waxwork figure squeezed between them, when Bonzo called after them.

"Hang on, there's something different about her," he said. "Turn around."

They turned really slowly.

Bonzo pointed his walkie-talkie at my waxwork figure.

"Her school uniform has gone. Why is she wearing a dress? I know that dress."

The silence was killing me. No one said anything for what felt like hours. It was probably only a few seconds, but I was hiding under a white sheet in a stuffy broom cupboard and the sweat was stinging my eyes.

I was literally going to jump to my feet and confess everything. I didn't want my friends to get into any more bother because of me. But a single word stopped me.

"VOMIT!"

Awful Agatha had really lost the plot now.

"What are you talking about?"

"Yeah, what are you talking about, Agatha?"

"Vomit! She was sick. She threw up over her school uniform. It was disgusting. So we found this dress in the museum."

"You stole it?"

"Lost property," said Charlie, speaking really quickly. "We borrowed the dress from lost property, after she threw up and, you know ..."

"Nearly died."

"Agatha, she didn't nearly die!"

Bonzo wasn't sure of their story. Who would be? It was getting more insane by the minute. Luckily, we all had one huge stroke of luck.

Bonzo was insane. "All right, get her some water and then tell your teacher what happened."

Bonzo slammed the door shut so I couldn't hear anything else. I was alone in the dark, but wasn't that concerned. I had time. Uncle Ernie always said that in a crisis, time was our best friend. As long as we had time to think about the problem, we could come up with a solution.

But I didn't have to. I heard the creaking handle. Light poured through the opening door. Uncle Ernie had found me. Together, I knew we'd be fine. We always were. I pulled off the white sheet and ran for the door.

"Uncle Ernie!"

"No, not Uncle Ernie."

I ran straight into the arms of the Cabbage Patch.

CHAPTER NINETEEN

It was funny. The Cabbage Patch's office actually smelled of rotten cabbages. He had insisted that the headmistress and I accompany him to his stinky office on the third floor, above the museum exhibitions and galleries. He sat behind a large desk made of oily timber, but it was full of maps, guides and coffee cup stains.

There was also a box of tissues. He kept snatching handfuls for his nose. He blew so hard his nostrils rattled. Sometimes, he pushed a long, bony finger into his hairy nostril, like he was digging through a sewer.

Even Miss Cannington thought he was repulsive. The old Cannibal pulled a face every time he shoved a finger up his hooter, looking for bogeys.

She sat beside me, which didn't exactly fill me with confidence. With the old Cannibal and the Cabbage Patch, I had no chance. It was two against one.

The Cabbage Patch slapped his notepad on the desk and picked up a cracked cup. The coffee turned his teeth brown.

"We need to get to the bottom of this, Miss Cannington. This girl has been giving me the runaround all day. First, she fainted in my Planetarium."

"Well, I would hardly say that's her fault, Mr Cumberlatch."

He raised a hand to silence the Cannibal, in the way that teachers do to little kids.

"Please, Miss Cannington. Let me finish."

He was disrespecting my headmistress. She got on my nerves and was soppy around Uncle Ernie, but I didn't like the way the Cabbage Patch was talking to her. I don't think he respected women. I don't think he respected anyone.

"As I was saying, she fainted in the Planetarium. She chased me through Future Earth and into the Royalty Exhibition. Then she gave me the slip at the Princess Power display before hiding in a cupboard at the Chamber of Nightmares."

The Cannibal didn't speak for ages.

"Sabrina. Is this true?"

"Of course, it's true," the Cabbage Patch interrupted. "And we know why, don't we, Sabrina?"

I wouldn't look him in the eye.

"Well, Sabrina? Will you tell your headmistress? Or shall I?"

"I don't know what you mean, Mr Cumberlatch."

He sat back on his leather chair.

"I'll tell you exactly what I mean. Miss Cannington, I have reason to believe that Sabrina isn't just a normal girl."

"I know she isn't," the old Cannibal said.

I couldn't believe it. She had known my secret all along, but had protected me. She was kind and caring and wonderful.

"Sabrina isn't a normal girl because none of my girls are normal. They are independent, resilient and open-minded. They are curious enquirers and confident communicators.

Every one of them is a unique individual, like a blooming flower in springtime."

"Yes, yes, I get the idea. I've got dinner plans this evening."

So the old Cannibal didn't know my secret. But she was about to.

"When I say, Sabrina isn't a normal girl, what I mean is she's not who she really is. I can show you something downstairs that will confirm who she really is."

"What?"

The Cabbage Patch leaned forward. He was really milking this. He even cleared his throat, ready to make his big speech, revealing who I really was, just like those detectives in predictable crime thrillers.

But he never got the chance.

His office door crashed open and banged against the wall. A cowboy stepped into the room. Well, he was dressed like a cowboy in an old movie. His blue jeans seemed pretty normal. And he wore a red checked shirt. But he had brown leather boots, a brown leather waistcoat and a tall, brown leather hat. He looked like he was wearing half a brown cow. He also had a big, bushy beard that reached his chest.

He touched the tip of his hat and nodded at Miss Cannington.

"Good day to you, ma'am. And what a mighty fine day it is."

He spoke funny, too.

"And how are you doing, little lady?"

He smiled at me. But he soon stopped when he turned to the Cabbage Patch.

"Cumberlatch," he said, shaking his head. "Cumberlatch, Cumberlatch, Cumberlatch."

The Cabbage Patch seemed totally lost now.

"I'm sorry, do I know you?"

"The name is William Thackery the third. Do you know who I am now?"

The Cabbage Patch started jiggling in his chair, as if he was sitting on ping pong balls. He straightened his tie and ugly blazer.

"You're Mr Thackery? *The* Mr Thackery?"

"I sure am."

Mr Thackery held out his hand and the Cabbage Patch shook it for so long, I thought their arms might fall off.

"It's a pleasure to meet you, sir. You are a legend in the museum industry."

"Ah, please."

"No really, you are. This is an honour, such a huge, huge honour."

The Cabbage Patch remembered that we were still in his office.

"Oh, ladies, Mr Thackery sits on the board of a dozen museums, including this one. I've never met him before, so this is a huge, huge honour."

Now he was repeating himself.

Mr Thackery helped himself to a chair and sat down.

"Ah, Cumberlatch, don't be all hat and no cattle. Maybe you should quit talking while you're behind. My granddaddy used to say that it's hard to put a foot in a closed mouth. Now, I'm having a meeting with your bosses later. But what's this I'm hearing about the chaos of your creation today."

"I don't understand, sir."

No one did. The cowboy had a funny accent and spoke in riddles.

"Every trail has puddles, son. And you've been leaving puddles all over this museum."

The Cabbage Patch looked nervously around his office floor. "I can assure you, Mr Thackery, there are no puddles, or any pools of water in this museum."

Mr Thackery whacked the desk top.

"You gotta stop taking everything so literally, son. I'm talking about a mess."

He pointed straight at the Cabbage Patch's pointy nose.

"And you've been leaving messes all over this museum like a horse leaves manure all over the prairie."

The Cabbage Patch was ready to burst into tears. It was brilliant.

"I don't really understand the bit about horse manure."

"You got missing exhibits, boy," said Mr Thackery.

"Ah, I see. Well, we found it, sir. It's back in the Princess Power display."

"And then you're scaring all our fine visitors with fake news about an insect invasion, something about a Norwegian Stop Watch Beetle."

"It's actually called the Norwegian Death Clock Beetle, sir."

"So it is a real insect?"

"No, it's a made-up insect, sir."

Mr Thackery rubbed his forehead. "Then what's the difference in its name?"

The quirky cowboy was obviously running out of patience.

"You got to get your game together, son. Stop worrying about fake beetles and fake missing exhibits. Do it right or get off the horse."

"What horse is that, sir?"

Mr Thackery slapped his own knee.

"It's an expression, Cumberlatch. Are you studying to be a half-wit?"

"No, sir."

"Then you were born a half-wit."

Mr Thackery stroked his enormous beard and winked at my headmistress.

"And what brings a beautiful young lady like you up here today."

The old Cannibal did that giggling thing she always does.

"Oh, beautiful, me, please. I wouldn't say beautiful."

"I most definitely would. You shouldn't be in Cumberlatch's old office when we've got so many fine exhibitions downstairs."

"Well, Mr Thackery."

"Please. Call me William."

"Certainly, William."

And she giggled again. The Cabbage Patch put his hand up.

"Er, can I call you William?"

"No, you can call me Mr Thackery. You can talk slowly, but think quickly. Then you can tell me why you're up here with these two young ladies, when you should be downstairs showing them round our magnificent museum."

"Well, Mr Thackery, there's an issue with this girl."

"What's the issue?"

"I think there are two of her in this museum, sir."

The Cabbage Patch sounded totally mad, which was lucky for me because he was the only one in the office telling the truth. Mr Thackery just sat there with his mouth wide open.

"So what are you telling me, son? She's got a twin in the museum?"

"No, sir, one of her is real. This one."

He pointed at me.

"I can see that, Cumberlatch."

"And the other one downstairs isn't."

"Isn't what?"

"Isn't real."

"What is it then?"

"Wax, like a candle." The Cabbage Patch laughed nervously. Mr Thackery muttered under his breath.

"Wax, like a candle," he said. "She's downstairs. She's wax, like a candle. That makes sense now."

Even the Cabbage Patch looked surprised.

"Does it, sir?"

"Yes, you're insane, Cumberlatch. The only issue here is your insanity. Stop wasting my time and get back to your tour guide duties. Or would you rather I discuss your candle wax twin sister thing with your bosses?"

"No, sir. Thank you, sir."

The Cabbage Patch scrambled to his feet and knocked his cracked cup over. The coffee dribbled onto his trousers. He looked like he'd wet himself.

"Oh, for heaven's sake, Cumberlatch, get yourself to the men's room."

"Yes, sir."

The Cabbage Patch couldn't get away fast enough. The cowboy held the door open for us and tipped his hat again.

"I'm sorry about that, ladies. Just ignore Cumberlatch. As my granddaddy used to say, 'Don't mess with something that ain't bothering you.'"

Once the old Cannibal was through the door and we were almost outside the office, the cowboy mugged me! He slipped his hand into my blazer pocket, pulled out my purse and threw it under the Cabbage Patch's desk.

"Tell her you've got to go back and get it," he whispered.

"Ah, Miss Cannington, I've left my purse in the office. I'll catch you up," I shouted.

The cowboy grinned at me like a cheeky schoolboy.

"So what do you think of my beard?"

"Yeah, it's good, Uncle Ernie. But your cowboy accent was rubbish."

CHAPTER TWENTY

Uncle Ernie tore off his fake beard. I had to be honest. The beard was fantastic this time. I knew who the cowboy really was straightaway, but I had to stay focused and pretend he was Mr Thackery. I even kept saying the name over and over again in my head.

Thackery, Thackery, Thackery.

I couldn't slip in front of the Cabbage Patch.

His cowboy accent was terrible though. He sounded like he was chewing a toffee.

But he had got the Cabbage Patch off my back and we now had a few seconds to organise our next move. That's why we talked so fast. We needed to return to the tour before the Cabbage Patch, Bonzo and my teachers became even more suspicious.

"So what's your big idea, Uncle Ernie?"

He stroked the beard in his hands, like it was a dead fox.

"It really was a great beard, wasn't it?"

"It was a bit too long. Where did you get it?"

"I found the lot in the storeroom. They must have had an American history section or something."

"That's brilliant. What do we do next?"

"I had to make the disguise convincing as he'd seen me around the museum as the pest control guy and the cleaner.

That's why I had such a good accent."

"It was a lousy accent. You sounded like you were chewing chocolate."

"I like chocolate."

"The plan, Uncle Ernie. What's the plan?"

He nodded a few times, as if he were clearing his head.

"You're right."

"Thank you."

"I need to work on my cowboy accent."

"No, we need to get out of here!"

"That, too. Right, I'll run downstairs and get to the waxwork figure before that buffoon Cumberlatch."

"But he's halfway there already."

My comments seemed to offend Uncle Ernie. He looked disappointed.

"You know, I was Mulakating's 100-metre sprint champion years ago, before you were born. In fact, I was thinking about the Olympics when ..."

"Yes, yes, yes, you're really fast, Uncle Ernie," I snapped. "You're the fastest man on the planet."

"Well, I wouldn't go that far. There was a guy from Jamaica."

"What about me?"

Uncle Ernie held my shoulders, but in the gentle protective way he does to show that he's taking charge, but he's also a bit worried about me.

"Go and get your purse under his desk, slowly. Count to twenty or something. Then get back to the Chamber of Nightmares. I'll have the waxwork figure out of the way by then."

"What about Bonzo?"

Uncle Ernie grinned.

"I'll have him out of the way, too."

I must have looked really scared because Uncle Ernie chuckled.

"Don't worry. I'm not going to feed him to the pigs. There aren't any pigs here."

"Uncle Ernie!"

"I'm kidding. You just get your purse and I'll take care of the other you."

He disappeared down the corridor, kicking off his cowboy boots along the way.

"And there was nothing wrong with my accent," he cried.

Even in the middle of the biggest catastrophe, Uncle Ernie never loses his sense of humour. He loses his mind on a regular basis, but never his sense of humour.

I tiptoed into the Cabbage Patch's office, counting each step towards his desk.

"One, two, three, I really need to pee," I whispered to myself. "Four, five, six, I've got a crisis to fix. Seven, eight, nine, I am committing a crime."

My silly rhymes helped me to concentrate and stopped me thinking about the disaster downstairs. I got onto my knees and crawled under the desk. Uncle Ernie was a great shot. The purse had slid all the way to the middle of the desk. I had to really squish myself into the tiny space. There were drawers on either side of me. The desk just had that one square-shaped gap in the middle for the Cabbage Patch to keep his sweaty feet.

I put the purse back in my pocket and tried to turn around. It was so cramped, I thought I might get stuck. I was worried I was going to rip my awful green blazer, which maybe wasn't such a bad idea. Most of all, I was just worried.

"Ten, eleven, twelve, I'm stuck in this stupid shelf."

I knew that *twelve* didn't really rhyme with *shelf*. And, yes, I also knew that I wasn't inside a shelf either, but I was nervous and my brain was doing somersaults and smashing against my skull.

"Hello, Bonzo, come in, Bonzo. Bonzo, you fool, answer the walkie-talkie."

I heard the voice first. Then I heard his footsteps. Then I saw his footsteps and those horrid green trousers of his ugly uniform.

Mr Cumberlatch had returned to his office.

Being squashed under his desk, I couldn't see any higher than his knees, but it was the Cabbage Patch, all right. Uncle Ernie always insists on a cool head in a crisis. I needed to stay still and think.

Of course, I couldn't do anything except stay still and think. That was the problem. I was trespassing under a horrible man's desk and the horrible man was standing right next to me!

Luckily, when I was little, I had had swimming lessons with Uncle Ernie, the only handyman in the universe who also taught young princesses how to swim. He trained me to hold my breath underwater, in case of an emergency.

Well, this was an emergency. I took the deepest, quietest breath and closed my mouth and eyes. That was the secret. I had to keep calm and carry on not breathing. Too much movement or panicking would affect my oxygen supply. So I thought about those swimming lessons back at the Palace and I kind of floated away to a happier place.

I stayed in my happy place for about five seconds when I felt a large thud above my head.

"There you are," said the Cabbage Patch.

I heard a clicking sound. He was pushing the button on his walkie-talkie.

"Bonzo, Bonzo, come in, Bonzo. Where are you now, you imbecile?"

There was loads of crackling on the walkie-talkie.

"Hello, boss, yes, boss, it's me, Bonzo," came a very dopey-sounding voice.

"I know it's you. Listen, I had to go back to my office for my notepad. Why haven't you answered me?"

There was more crackling on the walkie-talkie.

"Good news, boss, hur hur. I took them to the Tombs of Ancient Egypt."

"Yes, all right, that's your job."

"And they've all had a snack break and a toilet break."

"Yes, thank you, Bonzo, that is also your job."

"And I found that girl you were looking for, Sabrina."

The Cabbage Patch slapped his notepad against his desk top, making me jump.

"You haven't found her, Bonzo. I sent her back to the group."

"No, not her, the other her. The waxwork one that looks like her."

The Cabbage Patch's feet started skipping up and down. My heart started bouncing up and down. We were both going to flip.

"Why didn't you tell me that first?"

"Because I didn't find her first, boss. I took the students to the toilets first and that's where I found her, inside the family toilet. You're right, boss. She does look like that other girl."

"That's because it is her! I knew it. I've done some reading. Her home country is in the middle of a conflict. She's gone missing. There could be a reward for this."

"Reward for what, boss?"

"Her capture. Someone must want her in her country. They'll pay big money."

"But she's just a little girl, boss."

"Be quiet. She's a princess incognito."

"In where, boss? I've never heard of a country called 'Cognito'."

"Incognito, you nincompoop. She's from a royal family in hiding. You stay with the fake Sabrina. I'll get the real Sabrina. Put them together and I'll be rich."

His greedy, evil legs ran out of his office so fast, he didn't spot me hiding under his desk the whole time.

I was grateful for those swimming lessons at the Palace. Being able to hold my breath for so long meant that I didn't burst into tears.

CHAPTER TWENTY-ONE

I ran straight into a mummy. I wish it had been my mummy. But it was an Egyptian mummy, a dead queen from a long time ago wrapped up in bandages.

I knew how the poor woman felt.

I was turning into a hidden royal from a long time ago.

I had decided to head straight for the Tombs of Ancient Egypt, the next stop on our museum tour. If I had gone backwards to the rotten Chamber of Nightmares, I might have bumped into the Cabbage Patch, Bonzo or my other self.

And that's just what he wanted. The Cabbage Patch needed my waxwork figure and me together to reveal the truth. Maybe he'd take photographs and send them back to the Mulakating politicians who had a problem with my royal family. Maybe he'd stick me on Instagram or YouTube. Charlie already thought I was a YouTube star. And so did Awful Agatha now. That was another hassle to deal with later on.

But for now, I had to stay away from my waxwork figure. I couldn't let anyone see us in the same room, least of all that mean old Cabbage Patch. I'm sure he had already tried to Google me, but that was a waste of time. Uncle Ernie took care of the Internet. He had this data hacking program, which was all gobbledygook to me. I just knew that if anyone searched for "Sabrina Valence"—my real name— or "Sabrina Parslowe"—my fake name—or "Sabrina and Mulakating", then Uncle Ernie got this flashing alert on his phone.

He tracked the searchers. And then he blocked the searchers.

He really wasn't a regular handyman at all.

Luckily, the Tombs of Ancient Egypt was slightly closer to the Cabbage Patch's office than the Chamber of Nightmares, so I arrived first and pretended to be really interested in the Egyptian mummy stuffed in a glass case.

But I wasn't.

Back at the Palace, Miss Quick-Pants had taught the young royals all about the ancient Egyptians and the mummification process. That's what they did after they died. They wrapped the bodies to preserve them for the afterlife. But Miss Quick-Pants usually waffled on about the pharaohs, who were the kings and queens of Ancient Egypt, so it was boring. Doctors don't really want to learn about old, dead doctors, do they? Taxi drivers wouldn't want to read about taxi drivers from hundreds of years ago, would they? And I don't really want to hear about dead kings and queens, not with my own king and queen in so much danger.

Luckily, I'm a decent actor. I leaned over the Egyptian mummy and didn't move, as if she were the most fascinating museum exhibit of all time.

"There you are. I've been looking for you."

I felt a hand on my shoulder, but it was soft and gentle.

"Oh, hello, Miss Cannington. I'm just looking at this mummy. Do you know this one was embalmed and preserved almost four thousand years ago?"

The old Cannibal looked at me for ages.

"Hmm, you are a strange girl. You start the day by fainting, then I'm in the museum office with you for reasons that are still not clear and now you pop up using words like 'embalmed' and 'preserved'."

I knew exactly what to say.

"Yes, my Uncle Ernie says it's important to have a wide vocabulary. He makes me learn at least one new word every day. Uncle Ernie is your good friend, right?"

She wriggled around like she was being attacked by a load of wasps.

"Ooh, good friend, listen to you," she said, fanning her face with her hand. "I wouldn't say we were *good* friends, but we have a professional relationship and one thing in common. We're both concerned about your welfare."

She patted me on the head. She was lucky. If anyone comes near my head in a taekwondo class, I pin them to the mats. But I knew it was wrong to use my spectacular taekwondo moves on my headmistress.

"Anyway, you should re-join the class. Miss Shufflebottom is going to give a talk on the mummification process. It was supposed to be Mr Cumberlatch or that Bonzo, but they've gone to the toilet, at the same time, which is rather unprofessional if you ask me."

"Yes, Miss Cannington."

I had only walked a few steps, when she asked the question that I knew she was dying to ask.

"Has your Uncle Ernie said we are good friends then?"

I almost sighed sarcastically, but I remembered where I was and what an amazing actor I was. So I put on a really sparkly smile instead.

"Yes, Miss Cannington. All the time."

She adjusted her hair and giggled.

"I must arrange for him to come in on one of our parent-teacher coffee mornings. Of course, he can bring you along, too, Sabrina."

Only if I can bring along a sick bucket, I thought.

When I got back to the group, I saw the most amazing thing. Awful Agatha was paying attention again. She stood at the front of the group, next to Charlie, with her mouth wide open and her tongue hanging out. She looked like a komodo dragon.

Charlie was paying attention, too, but he usually did. Everyone was quiet, which was unusual because Miss Shufflebottom had a soft, timid voice. She spoke like she was permanently scared of everything.

It didn't make any sense.

"She's talking about dead people having their flesh ripped out," said Awful Agatha.

Now it made perfect sense.

Miss Shufflebottom was standing in the middle of two glass cases, each containing a coffin. The coffins were open and had a wrapped mummy inside.

"Now the Egyptians believed in life after death so they wanted their bodies to be cleaned and prepared for the afterlife," said Miss Shufflebottom.

She made us gather around the dead king. No one said a word. Even Liam stopped making rude noises.

"I'm going to talk about the seven basic stages of mummification. First the body was washed. Second, they removed the organs."

Awful Agatha threw up her hand.

"What kind of organ? A piano?"

Some of the other kids laughed behind their hands. Miss Shufflebottom looked confused, as she often did.

"What do you mean, Agatha?"

"You said they took away his organ, like his piano, right?"

Liam made the mistake of saying what everyone else was thinking.

"Do you really think an organ is a piano?"

"Do you really want a punch in the face?"

Awful Agatha was blushing, trying to use her temper to hide her embarrassment. She always did that. She looked to Miss Shufflebottom for help. "A piano is an organ, right, Miss?"

"Yes, it is, Agatha, but in this instance, I'm talking about organs of the body, like lungs and liver. Then third, the body was filled with stuffing."

I was impressed with Miss Shufflebottom. She was talking quickly. I could see what she was doing. She was moving away from Awful Agatha's awkward situation. That was a clever move for Miss Shufflebottom.

"Fourth, the body dried. Then the stuffing inside the body was replaced with linen. Then it was wrapped with pieces of linen, which look like bandages to us. And finally, the body was placed in a stone coffin, which is called a sarcophagus. Any questions?"

Liam raised his hand.

"Miss Shufflebottom," he said. "What happened to the piano?"

Everyone fell about giggling. It was quite a funny line, I suppose. Miss Shufflebottom nearly smiled. But then I noticed Awful Agatha's face. I had seen that face before, just a few times. It wasn't her typical face, which was always scrunched up and scowling. She was like a lost little girl, almost a baby. The tickle at the back of my throat vanished.

I knew what was coming next.

The face of the lost little girl always turned into the face of a raging monster.

Awful Agatha threw her rucksack to the floor. She pushed Charlie out of her way. He banged into the glass case, which made him fall towards the stone coffin, which left him face-to-face with the dead king's mummy. He cried out in terror.

Awful Agatha shoved her way through the crowd, which parted really quickly. No one wanted to get in the way of the raging monster. Miss Shufflebottom tried to grab Awful Agatha's shoulder, but Awful Agatha doesn't like being touched, by anyone, not even me, so that just made her even angrier.

She shrugged off Miss Shufflebottom and headed straight for Liam, who had stopped laughing, which was the smartest thing he'd done all day.

Liam was good at football and fast and sort of handsome, according to all the other girls. But he wasn't as big as Awful Agatha and he didn't know aikido and taekwondo like me.

Plus Awful Agatha hated his guts. She couldn't stand Liam because he was always trying to talk to me, which stopped me from talking to her. And I was the only proper friend she had. She had other girls hanging around her, but I called them hyenas. They weren't real friends. They just laughed at her bad jokes because they didn't want her to turn vicious. I was the only one who understood Awful Agatha, because we had a secret about our parents that we didn't like talking about. And Liam was always in the way. Plus, he had just made fun of Awful Agatha in front of the whole class. Twice.

Liam had no chance. He was going to get battered.

"I'm going to kill you. I'm really going to kill you, idiot."

"EVERYBODY STAND RIGHT WHERE YOU ARE!"

For the first time, I was almost pleased to hear the Cabbage Patch's posh, squeaky voice. He just appeared in front of the class. He sounded so furious that everyone froze, even Awful Agatha, which was lucky for Liam.

"Someone in this group is stealing our museum exhibits and that person knows exactly what I'm talking about."

And he looked straight at me.

CHAPTER TWENTY-TWO

Bonzo was in handcuffs. But they weren't proper handcuffs, like those metal ones that policemen use in the movies. They were grey, plastic handcuffs, the ones that come in cheap cops and robbers' sets for children.

He couldn't get them off.

He was standing in front of us, looking really tomato-faced, which I think was half-embarrassment and half-sweat as he tried to wriggle out of the handcuffs.

Mr Cumberlatch had never looked so angry. He kept staring at Bonzo and shaking his head. At first, we thought the Cabbage Patch had handcuffed Bonzo, which made sense. Bonzo would be really irritating to work with every day.

"I need your attention, we have a confidence trickster in the building," said the Cabbage Patch.

"Yeah, we also have a conman," said Bonzo.

The Cabbage Patch winced, as if he was sitting on a spike.

"A conman and a confidence trickster are the same thing, Bonzo."

"So there are two of them?"

Even Miss Shufflebottom was smiling. Bonzo never made much sense, but he looked even funnier trying to shake off a pair of plastic, toy handcuffs.

"No, there are not two of them. And why are you still wearing those handcuffs?"

Bonzo pulled one of his hands free.

"Ah ha! I am halfway there. These are really strong handcuffs."

"No, Bonzo, you are just exceptionally weak. Tell them what happened."

Bonzo cleared his throat, like he was going to make a long, important speech.

"I got handcuffed, hur hur!"

The Cabbage Patch smacked his own forehead in frustration.

"They know that, you fool. Tell them how you got handcuffed."

"Oh yeah, hur hur," Bonzo said. "Someone handcuffed me."

Everyone groaned. They wanted to get back to their mummies. So did I, but my living mummy in Mulakating. But I knew that couldn't happen so I was totally happy to let these two clowns waste time. That's what Uncle Ernie needed right now, loads and loads of time.

"No, Bonzo, the whole story," the Cabbage Patch said. "Trouble seems to be following this school around the museum and I want to know why."

His huge nostrils flared. He looked like a hippo.

Bonzo pulled his other hand free and cheered. But the plastic handcuffs flew across the Tombs of Ancient Egypt and pinged against a glass case.

That almost set off the museum alarms.

The Cabbage Patch stood with his hands on his hips.

"Are you ready now, Bonzo?"

"Yes, boss. I was standing outside the toilets looking after this waxwork ..."

The Cabbage Patch coughed loudly. Bonzo winked back at him.

"Oh yeah, that's right, Mr Cumberlatch, I'm not supposed to say waxwork, am I?"

The Cabbage Patch groaned really loudly this time.

"I was looking after something," said Bonzo, sounding really pleased with himself. "I was looking after something for Mr Cumberlatch, when a magician came over to show me a trick. He's doing a children's show in the museum later."

"No, he isn't, Bonzo."

"But he told me that he was."

"He was a confidence trickster."

"No, he was a magician. He told me."

"He was lying! He's been lying all day, running around the museum pretending to be pest control guys, cleaners and all sorts."

"All sorts of what?"

"Just get on with the story."

"So, yeah, right, there was this magician."

"Conman! He's a conman!"

The Cabbage Patch was shouting now. He needed to have a lie down.

"Yeah, there was this magician-conman doing magic tricks. And he asked me if I had ever seen the 'trapped hands' trick before."

The Cabbage Patch held his head in his hands. He moaned like an injured dog.

"I can't believe you fell for that trick."

"I didn't fall for it, boss. I stayed standing up. Anyway, the magician got out these really strong handcuffs."

"Toy handcuffs, Bonzo! They were toy handcuffs!"

"Yeah, well, he handcuffed my hands together and ran off with the wax—"

"BONZO!"

The Cabbage Patch's interruption sounded loud enough to wake up the dead mummies inside their tombs.

"Oh yeah, I'm supposed to lie, aren't I? Hur hur, I forgot. He ran off with the wax candles, outside the toilet, yeah, that's it, the wax candles. Did I do ok?"

The Cabbage Patch ordered Bonzo to pick up the toy handcuffs and started pointing at us, really aggressively.

"So you see, boys and girls, someone is making mischief in my museum."

Miss Cannington stepped forward. She actually looked quite cross, for once.

"Excuse me, Mr Cumberlatch. I hope you are not accusing anyone in this group. My school has been coming to this museum for years, with no problems."

"Yes, but classes change every year. You get new, *mysterious* students."

He was looking at me again. It was getting obvious. Even Awful Agatha and Charlie noticed it.

"You must keep a close eye on your new students. See

what they're up to. See where they've been, that kind of thing," said the Cabbage Patch.

He was heading in my direction.

"I've been a museum guide for schools for many years and I always find that if the behaviour changes at a particular school, look for what's changed at that school. Find the rotten apple."

He was almost certainly heading my way.

"There's always a rotten apple in every class."

He was definitely heading my way. Or he was, until little Charlie blocked his path. My best friend tilted his head right back, so he was peering up the Cabbage Patch's hairy nose.

"Where was this conman?"

"What?"

"Where was this conman, the fake magician?"

"What are you going on about, you tiny person?"

Charlie folded his arms. He was in no mood to be insulted over his height.

"I solve detective puzzles. Your conman was outside the Chamber of Nightmares, right? He stole something and then ran away. He's not going to follow you into the Tombs of Ancient Egypt, is he? A thief doesn't steal a wallet and then chase the victim. It's usually the other way round—he runs away. So your thief is not here. It's a simple process of elimination. So you're wasting your time being here. And we're wasting our time because we've got to leave soon and the map says we've only got one exhibition left. So can we move on, please?"

Charlie didn't even wait for an answer. He just marched past the Cabbage Patch. I was so proud of his confidence. He was getting all brave and assertive, just for me. I wanted to scream from the top of my lungs and tell the whole museum that he was my best friend and he used to be shy and scared, but now he was confident and bold and I was so, so proud of him.

But I just winked at him instead.

Charlie winked back at me with both eyes, which meant he couldn't see for a second and bumped into a mummy's coffin.

He still couldn't wink properly.

Awful Agatha followed Charlie, brushing past the Cabbage Patch.

"Yeah, move on, lanky," she muttered to the fuming museum guide.

He didn't know what to do. He didn't know what to say. The other students were walking past him and heading out of the Tombs of Ancient Egypt.

Even Miss Shufflebottom tapped her watch.

"Time is getting on, Mr Cumberlatch."

He had no choice but to leave the room and leave me alone. The leader had become the follower and Charlie had become the leader!

I waited for an extra second or two. I didn't want to be anywhere near that horrid man.

"Hey, Sabrina," said a quiet voice behind me.

The voice was coming from a stone coffin that was standing upright. The coffin lid was open. There was a wrapped mummy inside.

"Look behind, Sabrina."

I thought the mummy was talking to me.

I poked my head around the stone coffin. There was an arm waving at me. The arm was wrapped in bandages. It really was a mummy!

It was a mummy outside of its stone coffin, a mummy waving and talking to me. I'm supposed to be cool and rational and smart, but I was faced with a living, talking mummy.

I covered my mouth to stop myself from making loud, squeaky noises.

And then, Uncle Ernie's head popped up behind the mummy.

"What do you think? I've turned the other you into a mummy."

CHAPTER TWENTY-THREE

I had so many questions I was sure my head was going to swell and pop like popcorn in the microwave. How did Uncle Ernie carry the other me, the waxwork figure of me, into the Tombs of Ancient Egypt without anyone noticing? When did he turn the other me into a mummy? And where did he get those bandages?

I knew that he was the master of disguise, but this was crackers.

He was dressed as a museum guide and holding a bandaged mummy of a princess under his arm—a bandaged mummy of me!

I tried to reel off all my questions, one at a time, but my mouth couldn't keep up with my brain. I was talking gibberish.

Uncle Ernie tapped me on the head with a waxy hand from the other me, which was just surreal, but it did get me to concentrate.

"Pay attention, Sabrina, we haven't got much time," said Uncle Ernie.

"That's easy for you to say. This is bonkers."

"What is?"

I couldn't believe Uncle Ernie sometimes.

I poked a finger right into my eye, my waxy eye, not my real eye.

"This is bonkers, Uncle Ernie. This is all bonkers."

The bandages didn't feel like bandages. They were far too soft and easy to rip. I poked my waxy face again and felt my real face turning red.

"Uncle Ernie, what did you wrap me with?"

He laughed, but it was that silly, childish laughing.

"Ah, yeah, well, you see, what happened was, well, I had to grab you quick from the bathroom and I knew I had to run through here and, well, you know."

"It's toilet roll, isn't it?"

"That depends on how you define toilet roll."

"Is it toilet roll?"

"Yes."

"Uncle Ernie!"

The waxwork figure's frilly princess dress had vanished as well, which was unexpected. I even walked around the mummified waxwork figure to check. The dress was definitely missing.

"Where's my dress?"

"Ah, I couldn't wrap bandages..."

"You mean, toilet roll."

"Yes, that, well, I couldn't wrap toilet roll over a dress. It wouldn't look like a real Egyptian mummy. So I removed the dress and shoved it up my jumper. Didn't you notice my big belly?"

"Yeah, but I thought you had curry for lunch."

"Ooh, curry, yes, we'll have that tonight."

I was losing patience now. Uncle Ernie always protects

me, but he treats every disaster like it's a fun day out of the house.

"Did you take off the dress and cover me in toilet paper in the girls' toilets?"

Uncle Ernie looked appalled.

"Absolutely not. What must you think of me? I wrapped you up in the boys' toilets."

"That's disgusting!"

"How can it be disgusting?"

Uncle Ernie banged the other me on the side of the head with his knuckles. The waxwork figure sounded hollow.

"This isn't real," he said, banging the head again. "It's not really you, is it? And it's clean toilet roll. I almost run out and was going to look through the rubbish bins for extra paper."

I shoved my fingers in my ears.

"Argh! Don't tell me anymore. I don't want to hear!"

Uncle Ernie grinned at me. It was that goofy, boyish grin that showed off his bright teeth and always impressed women like Miss Cannington. It was the grin that my mum said made him look dashing.

To me, he looked dozy.

But I was secretly glad he was with me inside the museum.

"I'm only joking," he said. "Look we're almost there now. You'll be leaving soon and I can pop this back in the Princess Power display. And then, I'll come back, when the museum is closed, and I'll remove the waxwork figure for good. Or, to save time, I could set the museum on fire."

"Uncle Ernie!"

"It's a joke! Just get back to the group, get on the bus and get out of here."

"We can't yet. We've got one more exhibition left. Didn't you see Charlie lead everyone out of here?"

Uncle Ernie wasn't chuckling anymore. He pulled a map of the museum from his back pocket. He didn't seem pleased with me.

And then I wasn't pleased with me.

In fact, I was furious with me.

I was so obsessed with my naked waxwork figure being wrapped in toilet roll, I had forgotten about the bigger picture, the picture of the museum map.

It was shaped like a spider's web, where every exhibition led to the one in the middle, inside the grand hall, the biggest exhibition of them all.

"Oh no, it's the royal one," I said.

Uncle Ernie shook the waxwork figure.

"And *this* isn't *there*."

"No, it's out here wrapped in toilet roll."

Uncle Ernie took a deep breath and squeezed the waxwork figure under his arm tightly, like a rugby ball. The veins in his neck pushed through his wrinkled skin. Maybe he wasn't quite as strong as he used to be.

"Are you all right, Uncle Ernie?"

"I'm fine. I'll get this back into position. But you've got to come up with a diversion. Get there first, Sabrina. Do whatever it takes to stop Cumberlatch."

CHAPTER TWENTY-FOUR

When I was little, I thought I hated Uncle Ernie. And I mean real hate. The kind of hate that made me shout and scream and punch the pillow at bedtime.

I hated him because of the running.

Ever since I can remember, he had me running around the Palace. After kindergarten classes, he made me run around the sandpit. Sometimes, he even made me run in my diapers. Well, he called them nappies. Whatever they were called, I had to run in them.

I've seen the videos of me as toddler, waddling like a lunatic. I was quite a cute toddler, but no one wants to run around a sandpit all day. Sometimes, I made a mess of my diapers and kept on running.

After aikido and taekwondo classes, we ran together. After fencing and equestrian lessons, we ran together. After school lessons with Miss Quick-Pants, we ran together. After I had the flu, we ran together. Uncle Ernie called it recovery training. I called it really annoying.

He wanted me to be the fittest young royal, not just in Mulakating, but everywhere. I didn't even understand why. All I had to do was walk from some posh event to the car and wave at people and take their flowers.

But now I understood.

Even though my heart was bulging like a giant, red balloon, I wanted to find Uncle Ernie and squeeze him to death. Well, not literally squeeze him to death, that would be crazy. But I wanted to show him my gratitude for all the running and training—and vomiting, after that one time when he made me go jogging after I'd eaten three bowls of pasta.

Thanks to my genius Uncle Ernie, I wasn't just running now. Running was for wimps. I was floating. I was gliding like a beautiful white swan. No one stood in my way. They couldn't. I was too quick. I was like a blurry photograph. They could almost see me, but not quite. Museum visitors leapt out of my way, as if I were some sort of wild animal.

I was.

I was the cheetah, the fastest land animal on the planet, until now. Nothing and no one was catching me now, not even a cheetah.

I zigzagged through the museum's spider's web, moving from side to side like those skiers coming down a mountain in the winter Olympics. Uncle Ernie's words were ringing in my ears from just now, from yesterday, from every day of my life with Uncle Ernie.

Get there first, Sabrina.

I skipped past a family complaining about an Egyptian mummy looking fake because it was wrapped in toilet paper.

Get there first, Sabrina.

I legged it away from a security guard speaking on his walkie-talkie about a weirdo dressed up as a cowboy.

Get there first, Sabrina.

I spun around an old couple complaining about some pest control guy fogging them with his spray gun.

Get there first, Sabrina.

I squeezed through a group of tourists pestering a fed-up tour guide about the Norwegian Death Clock Beetles.

Get there first, Sabrina.

I was almost there. The archway was up ahead. I had been through that archway more times than anyone else in the museum, but I couldn't go through it again, not this time, not with the rest of the class.

That archway led to the Royalty Exhibition inside the grand hall, which led to the Princess Power display, which led to a waxwork figure of me, which wasn't there because it was wrapped in toilet paper and shoved under Uncle Ernie's sweaty armpit.

And then I saw them. They were hazy because everything was hazy. My feet were moving so quickly they were barely touching the ground. But I made out their bobbing heads. The vile Cabbage Patch and dopey Bonzo were at the front with Miss Cannington. Our green school blazers were in the middle, huddled together like a tin of peas, with Miss Shufflebottom at the back.

They hadn't quite reached the archway yet.

There was still time.

Maybe.

I ran harder, but it really felt like all the oxygen had been sucked out of the museum.

I couldn't breathe. I couldn't think. I couldn't even see straight. I was giddy.

But I blocked out all the noise, all the visitors, all the whining kids, all the tour guides speaking on megaphones, all the footsteps, everything.

Until there was just one voice left in my head.

Get there first, Sabrina.

I found an extra speed, just like on a bicycle when I click the handlebar to a higher gear. Every aikido warm-up, every taekwondo workout, every horse ride around the paddock and every embarrassing waddle around the sandpit in my diapers was helping me now.

I was almost there, overtaking the last of the visitors that stood between me and my classmates, past a shocked Miss Shufflebottom, past a blushing Liam and right up to Charlie and Awful Agatha, who were still leading the group towards my personal nightmare.

There was the archway right in front of us.

There was the sign that spelled my doom in dark, capital letters: ROYALTY EXHIBITION.

There was the faint outline of the other princesses in the distance, at the other end of the grand hall, with an obvious gap in the middle.

My gap.

My missing princess.

My missing life.

I almost fell on Charlie and Awful Agatha.

"Gotta stop," I spluttered.

I couldn't talk.

Charlie looked even more confused than usual.

"What?"

"Gotta stop, can't go in."

I wasn't making any sense. I couldn't find the right words. I couldn't really find any words.

I tried again.

"Stop them."

"Is it the YouTube star thing?"

"Yes. No. I don't know. Just don't go in. Please. *Please.*"

I was so tired and so dizzy that I didn't even see what happened next.

Awful Agatha punched me right in the face.

CHAPTER TWENTY-FIVE

I was dreaming. I had to be dreaming, or having a nightmare at least. This was madness. This was total madness. Normally my taekwondo would've blocked the punch, but I was already delirious from so much running. I just didn't see it coming.

Why would I see it coming?

Why would Awful Agatha punch me in the face?

She was my enemy once, but not anymore. Now, she was my friend, sort of. Why was my old enemy turning into my new enemy?

But I didn't have time to answer those questions. I was falling.

I hit the ground hard. My head bounced against the polished floor. I heard the screaming first. It was Charlie's screaming.

Then there were footsteps, leaping out of the way and then scurrying away from my face.

I was lying on my back when I saw the lights, high on the ceiling above my head. Why were ceilings in museums so far away? That was the strange question that popped into my head at that exact moment, which made no sense, but nothing else did either.

Suddenly, the lights were blocked. There was only darkness

and a scowling face. The darkness was real, but the scowling face didn't seem quite right. It didn't seem real.

Awful Agatha was coming towards me. All I could see was her long greasy hair and that scowling face. Her arms were reaching for my neck. She was going to strangle me. She was going to kill me inside the museum.

"What are you doing, Agatha?"

That was Charlie again. Or maybe it was Miss Shufflebottom. Or even Liam. The voice was so high-pitched and panicky that it could've been anyone.

Awful Agatha's hands soared towards me. Her fingernails were grubby. They always were. She never washed her hands properly at school. She never seemed to wash anything properly at home. No one at home cared about her hygiene.

Her fingertips were millimetres away from the tender flesh on my neck. I'd be squeezed like a chicken.

My throbbing brain had given up trying to make sense of the insanity, so my body took charge. My instincts took over. Uncle Ernie's training took over.

Uncle Ernie's running had got me here, just in time, before the class reached the Royalty Exhibition. I needed his self-defence training now.

I turned into a sausage roll. I was rolling, away from those strangling hands, away from the mad girl towering over my head.

Seconds later, I was on my toes, bouncing up and down, one foot in front of the other, holding my favourite taekwondo pose. My fists were up, protecting my face, ready for anything.

The children made a circle around us. No one had any clue what was happening, especially me.

Miss Shufflebottom had been at the back of the group. Miss Cannington had gone ahead with the Cabbage Patch and Bonzo. Charlie's wailing had got their attention. But they wouldn't arrive for another five seconds or so.

In a fight, five seconds was more than enough time to do serious damage. Five seconds could be a lifetime of pain and misery.

I took a step backwards, away from Awful Agatha, creating a delay, giving the teachers enough time to break us up.

But I was a split second too late. Awful Agatha launched herself through the air. She had completely lost the plot. Her move was so slow and so obvious that it was easy for me to swivel my hips and step to the side.

Maybe it was too easy.

Something was wrong.

As Awful Agatha lunged towards me, she did something that was truly nuts.

She smiled at me. And it wasn't one of those sarcastic, evil smiles that they make murderers do on terrible TV shows with lousy actors. It seemed like a proper smile. Her eyes were all bright and sparkly.

As she flew past me, she whispered something in my ear.

"Make it look real, you idiot."

"What?"

I leaned forward to reply, which gave her just enough time

to grab me in a headlock. With both arms, she tucked my held under her armpits.

But it wasn't a proper headlock. Apart from her sweaty armpits, the headlock wasn't uncomfortable. She wasn't squeezing hard enough.

Uncle Ernie's headlocks were much more painful. Normally, I'd throw a quick uppercut to the solar plexus, where all the nerves are behind the stomach. Uncle Ernie always told me to go for the solar plexus in an emergency. It knocks the wind out of an opponent really quickly.

My fist was clenched. My punch was ready to throw. I couldn't miss. Awful Agatha's stomach was right beside my head. If I swung my arm around, I had an open target.

But I hesitated.

She was barely holding me. Awful Agatha was not as tall as me, but probably had bigger muscles. She had to be stronger than this.

I felt her face on the top of my head. I could even feel her breath on my hair.

"Do your self-defence thing," she whispered.

"What?"

"Jeez, you really are dumb." Awful Agatha threw me to the floor.

"YOU KEEP MAKING FUN OF ME!"

She bellowed so loudly that all the other museum visitors turned around.

"I'M GONNA BOOT YOU RIGHT UP THE BUM."

Her grammar was dreadful, but her kick wasn't any better.

She swung her scuffed shoe through the air, but her laces barely touched my bottom. How could she miss from such a short distance?

I glanced up at her. She was still grinning like a lunatic.

"Fight back," she said, but she only mouthed the words, making no sound.

And then she winked at me. It was a proper wink with one eye, and my weary brain slowly started to wake up.

I scrambled to my feet.

"Yeah, well, you can't kick me in the backside," I shouted, loud enough for our teachers to hear.

"You can't call me a moron," replied Awful Agatha, even louder still.

"I didn't say you were a moron. I said you were an ugly moron."

"Yeah, well, you've got an ugly backside."

And like a couple of wild tigers, we pounced on each other and rolled across the polished floor together, waiting for the teachers to pull us apart.

As we wrestled around, our faces squashed against each other, which was lucky for both of us.

No one could see that we were trying so hard not to giggle.

Naturally, Miss Cannington arrived first. The headmistress yanked Awful Agatha to her feet. Then Miss Shufflebottom turned up, looking even more flustered than usual. She grabbed me.

"Get off me," Awful Agatha cried dramatically, shaking off the old Cannibal and flouncing around like an actress on stage.

"What are you doing, Agatha?"

"I'm killing her, Miss. That's what I'm doing. I'm going to kill her. She's lousy. This museum is lousy. You're all lousy."

The old Cannibal didn't know what to do or say for quite a while. She was genuinely flummoxed.

"I don't understand, Agatha," she said, after what seemed like ages.

Awful Agatha pretended to step towards me.

"It's easy, Miss. I'm going to kill her."

"Yeah, well, good luck with that," I shouted, gritting my teeth.

"No one is killing anyone," the old Cannibal said, holding us apart.

Awful Agatha rolled her sleeves up. She could be really dramatic when she wanted to be.

"I am. I'm killing her, Miss. I'm going to take her to the Chamber of Nightmares and stick her in one of those torturing machines."

Miss Shufflebottom sighed.

"Oh, Agatha, your imagination is always so vivid when it comes to violence. There wasn't a torturing machine in the Chamber of Nightmares."

"Yeah, well, I'll kill her with this then."

She threw her empty water bottle at me.

It sailed through the air.

It missed.

Everyone watched in silence as the water bottle bounced along the floor.

"That's enough Agatha, for heaven's sake," said the old Cannibal.

She was getting seriously cheesed off now.

"No, it's not enough. I wanna go home. She sucks. This museum sucks. This whole trip sucks."

The two teachers seemed to communicate with each other without speaking. They were fed up with the school trip, too.

I knew what they were thinking. Awful Agatha wasn't just humiliating herself. She was humiliating her school. She was humiliating her teachers.

Awful Agatha didn't really care about herself or her reputation. But the teachers had to care about the school's reputation.

The old Cannibal took a peek at her watch.

"Actually, it is getting rather late. Maybe we should return to the school bus and skip the Royalty Exhibition."

Everyone cheered.

Clearly, I wasn't the only one that didn't want to stare at royal waxwork figures.

I bent down to tie my shoelaces. I couldn't let anyone see the tears in my eyes. Crying was not allowed in school, not at our age.

But these were a different kind of tears, the kind I hadn't had for ages. They were happy tears, soppy tears really, but I wasn't bothered in the slightest.

I hadn't been this happy in a long time.

I finished pretending to tie my laces, wiped my eyes really quickly and sniffed.

When I stood up, Awful Agatha was being led away by Miss Shufflebottom.

She was still shouting about what a mean and horrible girl I was when she saw that I was staring at her.

She stopped shouting.

She gave me a sneaky thumbs-up.

So I gave her a sneaky thumbs-up.

And then she went back to shouting about what a mean and horrible girl I was.

CHAPTER TWENTY-SIX

The Cannibal made us sit on the naughty step. Well, it wasn't literally a naughty step. We were sitting on the cold, concrete steps outside the museum. But when I was in kindergarten at the Palace, Miss Quick-Pants made the misbehaved kids sit outside the classroom.

That was her naughty step.

This was my naughty step outside the museum, sitting beside Awful Agatha and being told off in front of the class.

At least they couldn't hear us.

They were on the other side of glass, with their mouths wide open, like goldfish. Miss Shufflebottom had taken everyone else back to the school bus, which was parked in the street, right in front of our naughty steps.

Charlie waved at me through the school bus window and patted the seat beside him. He had kept it free for me.

Five seats behind him, Liam was doing exactly the same thing, waving at me like he was the royal prince and I was a regular member of the public. If only he knew the truth.

He was also slapping the seat beside him. Both boys wanted me to sit beside them on the ride back to school.

Normally, I'd sit with Charlie. I always sat with Charlie. He was my best friend. But Liam had really tried to help me inside the museum, when that grotty Mr Cumberlatch was on my case. And when I thought about Liam, which wasn't very often if I'm being honest, I'd get this funny fluttering in my stomach. I wasn't sure if I liked him or I needed to use the toilet.

That's another headache for me to sort out later.

But normally, I'd sit with Charlie. So that was an easy decision. But today had been anything but normal. Today had been totally abnormal and ended even more abnormally, thanks to Awful Agatha.

Even now, she was making absolutely no sense at all, which was clearly irritating the old Cannibal.

"I will need to report this fight to your families, but I'm struggling to understand any of this," she said.

Our headmistress faced Awful Agatha.

"You've been so good and then, out of nowhere, you have a fight with Sabrina."

Then she turned to me.

"And you haven't been quite right since this morning when you fainted. Maybe I should've sent you home then."

It's a bit late now, I thought.

"I really don't know what to do with you two. But I'm very, *very* disappointed."

She made us wait on the naughty step while she trotted off to sign some museum papers for that vicious Cabbage Patch.

Awful Agatha and I didn't speak at first. She can't handle criticism, let alone praise, so I thought it was best to say nothing.

I was surprised when she kicked off the conversation. I was even more surprised with what she said.

"You're not a YouTube star, are ya?"

At first, I wasn't sure how to respond. I've been lying for so long that I can barely remember my true story from my fake one. I knew what Uncle Ernie would say. But he wasn't here. I was alone with someone who'd sacrificed herself to save me. Just like Uncle Ernie.

Suddenly, I wanted to speak to her in the same way that I spoke to Uncle Ernie. I wanted to tell her the truth, or as much truth as I could without anyone getting into trouble or danger.

"Nah. I'm not a YouTube star."

"But Charlie thinks you are."

"Yeah."

"Charlie's an idiot."

"No, he's not. He's kind. Like you."

She shook her head.

"No, I'm not. I'm Awful Agatha. Remember?"

"Yeah, all right. You're not kind, if it makes you happy."

"Yeah, it does. Idiot. So this stupid secret thing, are you a celebrity?"

"Nah."

Awful Agatha kicked a tiny stone off the step.

"Is it like me, then? You know. Family stuff?"

"Yeah."

"Yeah, well, I don't wanna talk about families, do you?"

"Nah."

"Families are boring."

"Mine isn't. They're just not here."

"Yeah, you're weird. You want yours here. I want mine to clear off."

Awful Agatha wouldn't look at me. I tried to smile at her.

"Why did you do that just now, in the museum? They might suspend you. You don't like being at home with your family."

She shrugged her shoulders.

"You wanted us to stop the class from going into that exhibition. So I stopped us."

I rubbed my cheek. It was still sore.

"You punched me in the face!"

"I'm Awful Agatha, right? Punching people is the only thing I'm good at."

"No, it's not. You helped me. You're good at that."

"All right, don't get soppy about it or I'll punch you in the face again."

"Yeah? Good luck with that."

We both giggled and then we stopped talking for a bit. The old Cannibal was taking ages. It was getting awkward. I decided to say something, even if it made my friend angry. I had to know the answer.

"But why did you pretend to fight me?"

"Stop going on about it, will ya? You're getting boring."

"But they'll suspend you and make you stay at home with your family."

Awful Agatha wiped her eye.

"My family don't give me cheese sandwiches every day, like you do. They don't give me anything. You're the only one who does."

She didn't need to say anything else. I understood what she meant.

I gave her a gentle nudge in the shoulder.

"I'll get Uncle Ernie to make you an extra one tomorrow."

"Yeah, you better. Make sure it's cheddar cheese. I don't like that dodgy cheese."

I really wanted to hug her, but I knew she'd probably punch me again.

"Yeah, I'll tell him, only cheddar cheese."

She rubbed her cheeks with her grubby green blazer.

"I'm getting on the bus. Charlie might have some food left in his lunchbox."

She skipped down the museum steps.

"Hey Agatha," I shouted after her. "Thanks."

She turned back.

"Stop being soppy, will ya?"

But I saw the tiniest smile escape through the corner of her lips.

By the time she climbed onto the bus, the old Awful Agatha was back. As she strutted down the aisle, she patted the girls' heads and pulled faces at the boys.

Weirdly, Awful Agatha was more like me than anyone else I knew.

We both pretended to be someone else every day.

Still, the day was ending better than I had expected, but that didn't mean I wanted to hang around this terrible place for another second.

I was halfway down the museum steps when I felt his bony hand on my shoulder.

CHAPTER TWENTY-SEVEN

"You're not going anywhere," said the Cabbage Patch. "I'm calling the police and they'll arrest you for stealing a museum waxwork figure."

I had almost made it.

I could see their faces through the school bus windows.

Charlie had his head down, solving another detective maths puzzle.

Liam was standing in the aisle, acting out another football goal for his friends.

Awful Agatha was pestering the other girls for food.

Everyone else was desperate to get away. Just like me.

"I don't know what you're talking about, Mr Cumberlatch," I muttered.

But we both knew that I was lying.

"Well, allow me to illuminate your dim memory. There is the small matter of a missing statue, taken from our Princess Power display, which looks just like you. The statue, which was made of wax, has been in and out of our Royalty Exhibition all day, just like you. Now why would that be? I think we both know why, don't we?"

"GET YOUR HANDS OFF MY STUDENT NOW!"

I froze.

The Cabbage Patch froze.

Even the pigeons on the museum steps seemed too scared to move.

The raging voice sounded like a volcano erupting. I was pretty sure I recognised the voice, but that only confused me more because she had never spoken quite so confidently before.

The Cabbage Patch still had his hand on my shoulder. We were both still frozen in terror, as if we were playing a game of musical statues.

"I SAID, GET YOUR STINKING FINGERS OFF MY STUDENT!"

I followed the voice to the top of the museum stairs and there she was, standing tall and with her hands on her hips like a superhero.

She stormed down the steps. Her back was straight. Her jaw was pointed. Her eyes were fiery. And her hands were still stuck to her hips.

I didn't recognise her.

She looked like Miss Cannington. But she didn't sound or behave like Miss Cannington. This was an alien Miss Cannington.

The Cabbage Patch finally took his hand off my shoulder.

That was a smart move.

He tried to defend himself.

That was a dumb move.

"Miss Cannington, please let me explain myself."

"No, you've had all day trying to explain yourself. All day, I've listened to you tell me how to manage my students, how to teach my students and how to keep my students entertained. Well, let me tell you, Mr Cumbersome ..."

The Cabbage Patch raised his hand.

"It's Cumberlatch actually."

"Not from where I'm standing, Mr Cumbersome. The only thing you got right was the bit about my students. They are *my* students, not yours, not the museum's and certainly not Bonzo's. They are *my* students and I know what they want and it's certainly not a feeble, petty, authoritarian bully like you."

"Now, look here."

She pointed a finger in his face.

"No, you look here, Mr Cumbersome. I have swallowed your patronising nonsense all day and I've just about had enough. And even more than that, I think you owe this young woman an apology."

"No, you don't understand, Miss Cannington."

"I understand perfectly, Mr Cumbersome. You are a bully. And we do not tolerate bullies at our school. Isn't that right, Sabrina?"

"Yes, Miss Cannington."

I thought I was flying, floating through the air. Luckily for me, I wasn't. Otherwise, I might have floated over to my beautiful headmistress and planted big, sloppy kisses all over her glowing face.

"I'm waiting for your apology, Mr Cumbersome, to me, to the school and most of all to this young girl that you've been picking on for most of the day. If you don't apologise, I will be forced to write a letter to your boss, Mr Thackery."

That really got the Cabbage Patch's attention. He bit his bottom lip.

"Sabrina," he said, really, really slowly. "Let ... me ... offer ... my ... sincere ..."

"Boss! Boss! I'm here, boss."

Bonzo came crashing down the stairs, bumping into visitors and carrying a walkie-talkie above his head.

The Cabbage Patch's mood immediately changed. He was back to his nasty, cocky self. His huge nostrils were flaring so much they looked ready to catch fire.

"Ah, Bonzo. Right on time. Did you go to the Royalty Exhibition?"

Bonzo was so out of breath that he made even less sense than usual.

"Exhibition, royalty, me, yes, boss."

"And did you go to the Princess Power display?"

"Yes boss, lots of princesses, lots of power."

Bonzo flexed his muscles to emphasise the power bit. He looked like an orangutan reaching out for a branch.

The Cabbage Patch gleefully rubbed his hands together.

"And did you find one of the princesses missing?"

I felt the blood draining from my face, as if someone had one of those enormous vacuum cleaners and was sucking out everything inside my head.

I reached out to grab Miss Cannington's elbow.

"No, boss."

I pulled my hand back.

"Thank you so much, Bonzo," the Cabbage Patch said. "You

see, Miss Cannington, a crime has been committed and ... wait ... what did you say, Bonzo?"

"No, boss."

"What does that mean? No, boss, there is no princess? Or no, boss, the princess is not missing?"

"Yeah, that one."

"What one?"

"Er, the middle one."

The Cabbage Patch stomped his feet like a toddler having a tantrum.

"Bonzo, there was no middle one."

"No, the princess wasn't standing in the middle, boss."

"Not that middle, I'm talking about the middle option."

"Middle optician? There's no optician inside. There are only princesses."

"Yes, I know that, Bonzo. Is one of them missing?"

"Who? The optician or the princess?"

"There is no optician!"

"So the optician is missing, boss! Shall I call the police?"

The Cabbage Patch looked ready to pull his hair out and maybe Bonzo's hair, too. He took a deep, slow breath.

"Bonzo, please, just listen, before one of us kills the other one."

"Yes, boss. I'm listening, boss."

"Are any princesses missing from our Princess Power display inside the Royalty Exhibition?"

"No, boss."

Now I wanted to kiss Bonzo. I really needed to get on the

school bus before I cuddled everybody on the museum steps, apart from that spiteful, skinny man.

The Cabbage Patch slumped backwards. It was his turn to sit on the naughty step. He deserved it, too. He just sat there, groaning.

"I have no idea what that was all about, but it's time to go," said Miss Cannington.

We hurried down the museum steps and ran across the pavement, only just missing an elderly street cleaner in a bright orange uniform. He kindly pushed his rubbish cart out of our way.

"Thank you, sir," said Miss Cannington, before running onto the school bus.

The elderly street cleaner touched the corner of his flat cap.

"You're most welcome," said Uncle Ernie.

CHAPTER TWENTY-EIGHT

My nightmare at the museum was over. I had left my other me, the waxwork version, in peace. At least one of us had been left in peace.

The real me was still at war, or my mummy and daddy were, back in Mulakating.

I was still living a fake life.

But this time, my real friends had saved my fake life. Uncle Ernie, Charlie, Liam and even the unbelievable Miss Cannington had helped me when I was in serious trouble with that rotten Cabbage Patch.

But Awful Agatha surprised me most of all. She stood up for me. She hadn't stood up for anyone else before. And now, she'll be punished for our pretend fight outside the Royalty Exhibition. We both will. Hopefully, she won't be suspended. I will make up some stuff. I'm a world champion when it comes to telling whoppers. Maybe we'll just have to stay back after school and tidy up the classroom or do extra homework.

The punishment won't be so bad, really. It'll stop us thinking about our families for a bit. And we'll be together.

That cheered me up as I climbed the steps of the school bus. I had never been so pleased to get on such a smelly rust bucket.

A funny little man stopped me at the top step of the bus.

It was Alan the Bus Driver. He stood at the front of the bus and made me wait beneath him. He towered over me. It was probably the first time in his whole life that he'd towered over anyone.

"Just wait there, please," he said to me.

He clapped his hands to get everyone's attention. He looked like a seal.

"Right, then boys and girls. I hope you all had a wonderful day at the Mayesbrook Museum of Modern and Ancient Wonders, but now you are back on my bus, where there is only one rule. What is my rule?"

He cupped his ear to listen.

"We must follow all your rules," we shouted back at him.

"Correct. And that means no eating, no drinking, no shouting, no singing, no spitting, no swearing, no fighting, no wrestling, no nose-picking, finger-flicking, hair-pulling or clothes-ripping, no peeing, no pooing, no kissing, no wooing, no farting, no burping, no vomiting, no slurping and no talking, especially no talking, unless it's an emergency, like one of you is on fire or something. Apart from that, you can do whatever you want. So sit back, relax and enjoy your trip back to school."

And the moment he finished talking, there was lots of eating, drinking, shouting and swearing, mostly from Awful Agatha.

Alan the Bus Driver squeezed his small body behind his huge steering wheel and waved me forward.

"Ok, that's my speech done. You can get on now," he said.

"Thank you, Alan the Bus Driver."

He picked up a flask of tea beside his seat.

"You're far too polite for this lot. It's almost like you don't belong here," he said, sipping his tea.

He peered through his windscreen. It started to rain. I tried to walk past him.

"Hang on a second," he said. "Do you like history?"

"Yeah, some of it."

I was eager to sit down. The museum was still beside us. That evil Cabbage Patch was too close for comfort. I wasn't interested in a dull chat with a stranger.

"I've loved history ever since I went to Egypt with my wife," said Alan the Bus Driver. "So I had a look around the Tombs of Ancient Egypt, all those mummies. It was superb."

"Yeah."

Not only was he a little man. He was a boring little man.

He sipped his tea. "Then I went to the Royalty Exhibition and saw all those young princesses on display," he said, looking directly at me.

My heart turned to stone, like one of those museum steps outside.

He took another sip of his tea.

"I read all about the history of Mulakating. It's such a beautiful place, but they're having so many problems with their royal family."

"Yeah," I croaked.

"There's nothing more important than family, eh?"

"No."

"Exactly."

Alan the Bus Driver finished his tea and smiled at me.

"So don't you worry, Sabrina," he said. "Your secret's safe with me, Princess."

THE END

Princess Incognito will return.

Princess Incognito's undercover adventures started with:

A Royal Pain in the Class

When Princess Sabrina of the House of Valence is exiled to a dull, working-class town, she must go undercover to keep her blue-blooded identity secret. Her parents, the king and queen, have sent her to a tough housing estate to keep her safe from the political troubles back home. Sabrina lives with her Uncle Ernie, The Earl of Parslowe, who has trained her to be an epic taekwondo expert. But even he can't prepare Sabrina for Awful Agatha.

The school bully hates Sabrina on sight and the two quickly become arch-enemies. Then, the princess meets her nemesis in a blockbuster showdown that forces them to realise they both have big secrets to keep and are more alike than they would ever admit.

Sabrina definitely has the right skills for a royal, but can she survive against Awful Agatha in the most rotten school in the world?

ABOUT THE AUTHOR

N. J. Humphreys is a bestselling author with 20 titles to his name. An engaging, witty storyteller popular with kids, he grew up in London and saw his first work published at 11, when he was picked to read his funny school journal to the world's toughest audience—hundreds of kids from his council estate. They laughed. He hasn't looked back since.

Among his many children's books, Humphreys' *Abbie Rose and the Magic Suitcase* series are entertaining eco-adventures about a smart, feisty girl on a mission to save endangered animals. He is currently working on the animated TV series with an international broadcaster.

He is based in Singapore.